The Sorceress' Claim
The Shadow Sisters – Book One

Written by Miche

Copyright © Michelle Mackenzie 2024

Published by Quill & Fury Publishing

All rights reserved. No part of this publication may be reproduced, stored or transmitted in any form or by any means, electronic, mechanical, photocopying, recording, scanning, or otherwise without written permission from the publisher. It is illegal to copy this book, post it to a website, or distribute it by any other means without permission.

Disclaimer

This novel is entirely a work of fiction. The names, characters and incidents portrayed in it are the work of the author's imagination. Any resemblance to actual persons, living or dead, events or localities is entirely coincidental.

M. V Mackenzie has no responsibility for the persistence or accuracy of URLs for external or third-party Internet Websites referred to in this publication and does not guarantee that any content on such Websites is, or will remain, accurate or appropriate.

Designations used by companies to distinguish their products are often claimed as trademarks. All brand names and product names used in this book and on its cover are trade names, service marks, trademarks and registered trademarks of their respective owners. The publishers and the book are not associated with any product or vendor mentioned in this book. None of the companies referenced within the book have endorsed the book.

Chapter 1

Samantha stood in front of her bathroom mirror, carefully applying her makeup. She wanted to look perfect for her anniversary dinner with her boyfriend, Ethan. It had been two years since they started dating, and tonight was a special occasion.

Samantha studied her reflection, ensuring her eyeliner was even and her lipstick was flawless. She ran a hand through her long, dark hair, making sure it fell in soft waves around her face. Satisfied with her appearance, she stepped back and smiled.

"Time to get dressed," she said, turning and walking into her bedroom. She had picked out the perfect outfit - a sleek black dress that hugged her curves and showed off her long legs. She slid the dress on, smoothing the fabric over her hips. Samantha finished the look with a pair of stripey black heels and a delicate silver necklace.

Glancing at the clock, Samantha saw that it was just after 6 pm. Their dinner reservation was for 7, so she still had plenty of time to get to the restaurant. She grabbed her small purse and headed out the door, locking it behind her.

The drive to the restaurant was uneventful. Samantha hummed along to the radio, excitement bubbling inside her. She couldn't wait to see Ethan and celebrate their anniversary. When she pulled up to the restaurant, she double-checked the time - 6:45 pm. Perfect.

Samantha walked through the front doors, immediately spotting the hostess stand. "Hi, I have a reservation for two under the name Samantha," she said with a smile.

The hostess checked her list and nodded. "Right this way, ma'am." She grabbed two menus and led Samantha through the dimly lit dining room.

Their table was in a quiet corner, and Samantha slid into the plush booth, setting her purse down next to her. "Thank you," she said to the hostess, who nodded and left Samantha alone.

Samantha glanced around, expecting to see Ethan arrive at any moment. But as the minutes ticked by, he was nowhere to be seen. She frowned, pulling out her phone to send him a quick text.

"Hey babe, I'm here. Where are you?"

She waited, watching the screen, but no response came. Samantha sighed and placed the phone back in her purse, trying not to let her worry show. Ethan was usually very punctual - he hated being late. Maybe he was just running a little behind.

The waiter came by, and Samantha ordered a glass of red wine, hoping it would help calm her nerves. As she sipped the rich, full-bodied liquid, her eyes kept darting to the entrance, waiting for Ethan to walk through the doors.

But he didn't.

By the time her glass was empty, an hour had passed. Samantha stared down at the white tablecloth, her heart sinking. Where was he? This wasn't like him at all. She pulled out her phone again, this time calling his number. It rang several times before going to voicemail.

"Ethan, it's me. Where are you? I'm at the restaurant waiting. Please call me back as soon as you can." Samantha ended the call, her brow furrowed in concern.

The waiter returned, asking if she would like another glass of wine. Samantha hesitated, then nodded. "Yes, please." As the waiter walked away, she glanced around the restaurant, watching as other couples and groups chatted and laughed, completely unaware of her distress.

The second glass of wine went down just as quickly as the first. By now, it was after 8 pm and Samantha's stomach was in knots. She couldn't understand what was keeping Ethan. It just wasn't like him to be this late or unresponsive.

"Excuse me, is everything alright?" the waiter asked, approaching the table again.

Samantha looked up, forcing a small smile. "Oh, yes, I'm fine. I'm just waiting for my boyfriend to join me."

The waiter glanced at the empty seat across from her. "I see. Well, please let me know if there's anything I can get you in the meantime."

"Thank you," Samantha replied, taking another sip of her wine.

As the evening wore on, Samantha became more and more uneasy. Where was Ethan? Why wasn't he answering his phone? She wracked her brain, trying to think of any reason he could be this late or unreachable. But nothing came to mind.

Finally, at nearly 9:30 pm, Samantha could no longer sit still. She pushed her chair back and stood up, grabbing her purse. "I'm sorry, but I need to go," she told the waiter. "Please just put the wine on my bill."

The waiter nodded, looking concerned. "Of course, ma'am. I hope everything is alright."

Samantha forced another tight-lipped smile. "I'm sure it is. Thank you." She hurried out of the restaurant, her heels clicking against the tile floor.

Once outside, Samantha pulled out her phone again, dialling Ethan's number. This time, it went straight to voicemail. "Ethan, where are you? I'm leaving the restaurant now. Please, just call me back. I'm worried about you." She ended the call, her brow furrowed in concern.

Samantha walked quickly to her car, her mind racing. Something was wrong, she could feel it. Ethan would never stand her up like this without at least letting her know what was going on. As she slid into the driver's seat and started the engine, a sense of dread settled in the pit of her stomach.

Without a second thought, Samantha drove to Ethan's apartment. The short trip felt like an eternity as she worriedly tapped her fingers against the steering wheel. When she pulled up to the familiar building, she hurried inside and up the stairs to his door.

Samantha raised her hand to knock but paused. What if he was fine and she was just overreacting? She didn't want to seem like a crazy, overbearing girlfriend. Taking a deep breath, she pressed the doorbell and waited.

No answer.

She tried knocking again, louder this time. Still no response. Samantha's heart raced as she pulled out her phone and called Ethan's number once more. This time, it rang and rang, but there was no answer.

"Ethan, please pick up," Samantha pleaded, her voice barely above a whisper. When the call went to voicemail again, she felt a wave of panic wash over her. Something was wrong, she was sure of it.

Without a second thought, Samantha hurried back down the stairs and jumped into her car. She needed to find Ethan, and she needed to find him now. As she drove, she wracked her brain, trying to think of anywhere he might be. His work? The gym? A friend's house? But no matter where she went, she had a sinking feeling that she wouldn't find him.

After nearly an hour of fruitless searching, Samantha found herself driving aimlessly through the dimly lit streets of the city. The panic and worry she felt had given way to a growing sense of dread. Where could he be? What had happened to him?

She arrives home at almost midnight. She was probably overreacting. Knowing him, he'd forgotten the day and slept through his alarm again. She helped herself to a glass of wine from her steel fridge and sighed. She peeled the clothes from her tired limbs and stepped into a hot shower. Half an hour later, she climbed into bed. Her last thoughts were about him.

Chapter 2

Samantha awoke the next morning with a sense of unease. After hours of fruitlessly searching for Ethan the previous night, she had finally given in to exhaustion and returned home, her mind racing with worry and uncertainty.

As she lay in bed, the events of the night before replaying in her mind, Samantha knew she couldn't just sit around and wait for Ethan to make contact. Something had to be wrong - it was so unlike him to simply disappear without a word.

With a determined sigh, Samantha pushed herself out of bed and quickly got dressed. She needed to go to Ethan's apartment and find out what had happened. Maybe he had simply overslept or lost track of time. Or maybe...

Samantha pushed the darker thoughts from her mind, refusing to entertain them. Ethan was fine, he had to be. She just needed to see him, to make sure he was alright.

The drive to Ethan's apartment felt agonizingly long, and Samantha's nerves were on edge the entire way. When she finally pulled up to the familiar building, she hurried inside and practically ran up the stairs to his front door.

Taking a deep breath to calm her racing heart, Samantha knocked loudly, listening intently for any signs of movement from within. After a moment, she heard the sound of footsteps approaching, and the door swung open to reveal a dishevelled-looking Ethan.

"Ethan!" Samantha exclaimed, relief flooding through her. "I've been so worried! Where were you last night? I waited for hours at the restaurant."

Ethan blinked at her, his expression puzzled. "Restaurant? What are you talking about?"

Samantha stared at him, confusion etched across her face. "Our anniversary dinner, remember? I got all dressed up and everything."

Ethan's eyes widened with realization. "Oh god, Samantha, I'm so sorry. I completely forgot about that. I must have slept through my alarm or something." He raked a hand through his messy hair, looking utterly dismayed.

Samantha felt a flicker of unease. "Slept through your alarm? Ethan, that's not like you at all. Is everything okay?"

He offered her a sheepish smile. "Yeah, yeah, I'm fine. I just...I must have been more tired than I realized. Come on in, I'll make it up to you."

Samantha hesitated for a moment, her gaze searching his face for any signs of deception. But Ethan seemed genuinely apologetic, and she couldn't detect any hint of malice or dishonesty in his expression.

With a small nod, she stepped past him into the apartment, her eyes quickly scanning the familiar surroundings. Everything seemed to be in order - no signs of a struggle or any indication that something might be amiss.

"Can I get you some coffee or something?" Ethan asked, closing the door behind her.

The Sorceress' Claim

"Coffee would be great, thanks," Samantha replied, her gaze still roaming the room.

As Ethan moved into the kitchen, Samantha's eyes fell on his phone, sitting on the coffee table. The screen was lit up, and Samantha couldn't help but notice the name "Maggie" displayed prominently.

Her heart skipped a beat, and a cold knot of dread began to form in the pit of her stomach. Maggie was her best friend - what could she possibly be doing contacting Ethan?

Before Samantha could think too deeply about it, Ethan returned with two steaming mugs of coffee. "Here you go," he said, handing one to her.

Samantha accepted it gratefully, but her mind was still racing. "Ethan, I...I saw a notification on your phone. From Maggie."

Ethan's expression shifted ever so slightly, and Samantha thought she saw a flicker of panic in his eyes. "Oh, that? It was probably just...you know, girl stuff. Nothing important."

Samantha narrowed her eyes, sensing that he was hiding something. "Ethan, what's going on? Why would Maggie be contacting you?"

He shifted uncomfortably, his gaze dropping to the floor. "It's...it's nothing, really. We've just been talking, that's all."

"Talking?" Samantha felt a rising sense of dread. "About what?"

Ethan sighed heavily, finally meeting her gaze. "Look, Samantha, I...I haven't been completely honest with you."

Samantha felt her heart drop, the memories of the previous night's betrayal flooding back. "What are you saying, Ethan?"

"I...I've been seeing Maggie. Behind your back." Ethan's voice was barely above a whisper, his eyes filled with shame.

Samantha stared at him, her mind reeling. This couldn't be happening. "No," she breathed, the word escaping her lips in a pained whisper. "No... Tell me you're joking."

Ethan reached out to her, but Samantha recoiled, her eyes narrowing in a mix of hurt and fury. "Don't touch me," she hissed. "How could you do this to me?"

"Samantha, I'm so sorry," Ethan pleaded, his own eyes glistening with tears. "It just...it just happened. I never meant to hurt you."

Samantha felt a surge of rage coursing through her veins, drowning out the pain and betrayal. "You're a liar," she spat.

Ethan flinched at her sharp tone. "It's not like that, Samantha. I swear."

"Bullshit!" Samantha shouted, her voice trembling with emotion. "You both betrayed me and with my own best friend, no less."

Ethan opened his mouth to speak, but before he could, a knock at the door interrupted them. Samantha's heart pounded in her chest as Ethan moved to answer it, a sinking feeling in the pit of her stomach.

When the door swung open, Samantha felt her world tilt on its axis. Standing there, a guilty expression on her face, was Maggie.

"Maggie," Samantha breathed, her voice laced with disbelief and betrayal.

"Samantha," Maggie replied, her own voice barely above a whisper. "I...I'm so sorry."

Samantha felt a surge of rage coursing through her. Without a second thought, she lunged forward, her fist connecting with Maggie's face with a sickening crack. Maggie stumbled back, clutching her now-bleeding nose, but Samantha didn't stop there.

She pushed past Ethan, her hands reaching for Maggie's throat. "How could you do this to me?" she screamed, her vision blurred by tears of anguish and fury.

Maggie gasped and choked, her own hands frantically clawing at Samantha's, but Samantha didn't relent. All she could think about was the pain and heartbreak they had caused her, and she was determined to make them pay.

Ethan tried to pull Samantha off of Maggie, but Samantha lashed out, her elbow connecting with his ribs. He grunted in pain but didn't let go.

"Samantha, stop!" he shouted, his voice laced with desperation. "This isn't going to solve anything!"

But Samantha couldn't hear him, her mind consumed by a red haze of rage. She continued to squeeze Maggie's throat, her grip tightening with each passing second.

Maggie's struggles grew weaker, and Samantha could hear the gurgling sounds of her desperate gasps for air. Just as she thought she might finally succumb to the darkness, Ethan managed to pry her off, his own face contorted with a mix of fear and anguish.

Samantha staggered back, her chest heaving, and stared at the two of them, her expression a twisted mask of heartbreak and betrayal.

"I hate you," she spat, the words dripping with venom. "Both of you. I never want to see your faces again."

Without another word, Samantha turned and fled the apartment, her mind reeling, her heart shattered beyond repair. She had to get out of there, she couldn't bear to be in the same room as the two people who had betrayed her so utterly and completely.

As she raced down the stairs and out to her car, Samantha felt a sense of despair and utter hopelessness wash over her. How could this be happening again? How could the people she trusted most in the world do this to her?

Tears streamed down her face as she drove aimlessly through the city, her mind consumed by a maelstrom of emotions. She had lost everything - her boyfriend, her best friend, her sense of security and trust.

Samantha drove through the city streets, her vision blurred by tears of anguish and betrayal. She couldn't believe what had just happened - how could the two people she trusted most in the world have done this to her, again?

The pain and heartbreak were overwhelming, and Samantha could barely focus on the road ahead of her. She needed to get away, to put as much distance between herself and Ethan and Maggie as possible.

As she turned a sharp corner, Samantha suddenly lost control of her car. The wheels screeched as she swerved, and the vehicle careened off the road, slamming into a stone wall with a deafening crash.

Samantha cried out in pain as her head slammed against the window, and everything went black.

Chapter 3

When she finally came to, Samantha found herself lying on the cold, hard ground, disoriented and in agony. She tried to move, but a searing pain shot through her side, and she let out a pained gasp.

"Easy there, dear," came a soft, soothing voice. "You've been through quite an ordeal."

Samantha blinked, her vision slowly coming into focus. A woman with striking, violet-coloured eyes and long, Ashley-black hair was kneeling beside her, a concerned expression on her face.

"Who...who are you?" Samantha managed to croak, her throat dry and raw.

"My name is Trixie," the woman replied, her voice warm and gentle. "I found you unconscious by the side of the road. You were in a terrible accident."

Samantha furrowed her brow, trying to piece together what had happened. "I...I don't remember," she whispered, the realization dawning on her.

Trixie nodded solemnly. "It seems you've suffered a head injury. Don't worry, dear, that's not uncommon after a trauma like this. But the good news is, you're alive."

Samantha looked up at the woman, her eyes filled with a mixture of fear and confusion. "What am I going to do? I don't know who I am or where I came from."

Trixie reached out and gently squeezed her hand. "Don't worry, my dear. I'll take care of you. You can come stay with me and my friends - we'll help you get back on your feet."

Samantha searched Trixie's face, longing for some sense of familiarity or reassurance. "Your...friends?"

"Yes, the Shadow Sisters," Trixie replied with a warm smile. "We're a close-knit group, and we look after one another. You'll be safe with us."

Samantha hesitated, her mind racing. She had no idea who this Trixie woman was or what she was getting herself into. But the alternative - being alone and lost in the world with no memories - was far more terrifying.

With a resigned nod, Samantha accepted Trixie's offer. "Okay. I...I'll come with you."

Trixie's smile widened, and she gently helped Samantha to her feet, supporting her as they made their way to a nearby car. "Don't worry, my dear. Everything is going to be just fine."

As they drove through the city, Samantha stared out the window, her mind a whirlwind of unanswered questions. Who was she? Where did she come from? And what had happened to her?

But as the car pulled up to a large, imposing-looking house, Samantha pushed those thoughts aside. For now, she would have to trust in Trixie and her mysterious "Shadow Sisters." It was the only choice she had.

Samantha followed Trixie up the winding path to the entrance of the impressive, gothic-style mansion. As they approached the large, ornate doors, Trixie paused and turned to Samantha with a reassuring smile.

"Welcome to our humble abode, my dear," she said, reaching out to gently squeeze Samantha's hand. "Don't be nervous - the girls are eager to meet you."

Samantha nodded, trying to muster a small smile, though her heart was racing with a mixture of trepidation and curiosity. She had no idea what to expect from these "Shadow Sisters" Trixie had mentioned, but the woman's warm and welcoming demeanour had put her somewhat at ease.

As Trixie pushed open the doors, Samantha's gaze swept across the grand, dimly lit foyer. Elegant, antique furnishings adorned the space, casting long shadows across the polished marble floor. Samantha couldn't help but feel a sense of unease creeping up her spine, but she pushed it down, determined to give these strangers a chance.

"Trixie, darling, you're home!" a voice suddenly called out, and Samantha's eyes were drawn to the top of a grand staircase where a striking woman with porcelain skin and jet-black hair was descending. "And you've brought a guest!"

The woman glided down the stairs with feline grace, her striking features and piercing gaze immediately captivating Samantha. As she approached, Samantha caught a glimpse of a peculiar tattoo on the woman's wrist - a crescent moon surrounded by three stars.

"Girls, come meet our new friend!" the woman called out, her ruby-red lips curving into a mysterious smile.

Suddenly, two more women appeared, seemingly materializing out of the shadows. One was tall and willowy, with sharp, angular features and striking green eyes, while the other was petite and delicate, with a mane of fiery red curls.

"This is... well, we don't know. She was in a car accident, so she doesn't remember who she is," Trixie said, wrapping an arm around Samantha's shoulders in a gesture of comfort and support. "She's been through a terrible ordeal, and we're going to take care of her."

The three women gathered around Samantha, their eyes roaming over her curiously. Samantha felt a shiver of unease run down her spine, but she forced herself to stand tall, meeting their gazes with as much confidence as she could muster.

"It's a pleasure to meet you," the Ashley-haired woman said, her voice smooth and alluring. "I'm Ashley, and these are my sisters, Jade and Ember."

Jade, the tall, green-eyed beauty, stepped forward and offered Samantha a warm smile. "Welcome to our home. We're so glad you're here."

Ember, the petite redhead, flashed Samantha a dazzling grin. "Yes, welcome! We're going to have so much fun together."

Samantha felt a small, tentative smile tug at the corners of her lips. These women, while certainly enigmatic, seemed genuinely welcoming and kind. Perhaps staying with them wouldn't be so bad after all.

"Thank you, all of you," she replied, her voice soft but sincere. "I...I don't know what I would have done without Trixie's help."

Ashley nodded, her gaze appraising. "Well, you needn't worry about that anymore, my dear. You're safe here with us."

Trixie gave Samantha's shoulder a gentle squeeze. "Come, let's get you settled in. I'm sure you must be exhausted."

Samantha followed the four women up the grand staircase, her curiosity piqued. As they reached the top landing, Ashley turned to her with a warm smile.

"This way. We've prepared a room for you."

Samantha trailed behind the group, her eyes drawn to the intricate tapestries and ornate chandeliers adorning the hallway. The entire mansion exuded an air of mystery and power, and Samantha couldn't help but feel a strange sense of foreboding.

Yet, as Ashley ushered her into a cosy, dimly lit bedroom, Samantha felt a wave of relief wash over her. The room was warmly furnished, with a plush bed and a large, ornate mirror that seemed to catch the flickering candlelight.

"Rest now, my dear," Ashley said, her voice soft and soothing. "We'll be downstairs if you need anything."

Samantha nodded, sinking onto the edge of the bed. As the four women turned to leave, she couldn't help but call out, "Thank you, all of you. I…I don't know what I would do without your kindness."

Ashley paused, a mysterious smile playing on her lips. "Think nothing of it, Samantha. We're family now."

With that, the women departed, leaving Samantha alone in the shadowy room. As she lay back against the pillows, her mind swirling with questions and uncertainty, Samantha couldn't shake the feeling that her life had just taken an unexpected turn.

The full moon shone against the blanket of stars. The branches of nearby trees brushed against the windows of her room. Samantha buried her head into the quilt and shivered from the cold.

After listening to the sounds of nature and the leaves rustling, she finally drifted off into a troubled sleep. Fragments of memories that she couldn't quite grasp haunted her dreams until she woke up with the rising sun and a knock on the bedroom door.

Chapter 4

The morning rays of sunlight filtered through the ornate, stained-glass windows, casting a warm glow over the large, opulent bedroom. Samantha stirred, blinking her eyes open as she took in her surroundings.

It all felt so foreign and unfamiliar, a stark contrast to the fuzzy, fragmented memories that had haunted her dreams. Try as she might, she couldn't recall anything concrete about her past or who she truly was.

With a soft sigh, Samantha pushed herself up into a sitting position, her gaze drifting towards the ornate mirror that dominated one wall of the room. Staring back at her was a face she didn't recognize, filled with uncertainty and a hint of fear.

Suddenly, the sound of raised voices from beyond the bedroom door caught her attention, and Samantha strained to listen.

"I don't understand why you didn't take her to the hospital, Trixie," a sharp, clipped voice said. "What if she's dangerous?"

Samantha's brow furrowed as she recognized the voice as belonging to the dark-haired woman, Ashley.

"You know as well as I do that the doctors wouldn't have been able to help her," Trixie replied, her own tone laced with a hint of exasperation. "Her mind has been wiped clean - she has no memories, no identity. We're the only ones who can help her now."

"But what if she's not who she seems?" a second, more melodic voice chimed in. "What if she's some kind of...spy or infiltrator, sent here to uncover our secrets?"

Samantha's heart began to race as she realized they were talking about her. Spy? Infiltrator? The words sent a chill down her spine.

"Jade, darling, you worry too much," Trixie said, her voice soothing. "Samantha is lost and alone. We have a responsibility to help her, to guide her. She's one of us now."

"I still don't like it," a third, fiery voice piped up. "What if she's dangerous? What if she poses a threat to our coven?"

Samantha's eyes widened in alarm. Coven? These women were more than just a close-knit group of friends - they were...witches? Sorceresses?

"Ember, you know as well as I do that we are more than capable of handling any threat," Ashley's commanding voice replied. "And besides, Trixie has assured us that the girl poses no danger. We will keep a close eye on her, but we will not turn our backs on her."

Samantha's heart was pounding in her chest as the realization dawned on her. These women had taken her in, despite their misgivings, because they believed they could help her. But what did that mean, exactly? And what did they expect from her in return?

As the women's voices faded, Samantha's gaze drifted back to the mirror, her brow furrowed in deep thought. She had to get to the bottom of this, to uncover the truth about her rescuers and their true intentions.

Just as she was about to push herself out of the bed, a sudden movement in the mirror caught her eye. Startled, Samantha jumped, and in the process, her elbow caught the edge of an ornate vase, sending it crashing to the floor.

The sound of shattering glass echoed through the room, and Samantha froze, her heart pounding in her ears. Moments later, the bedroom door flew open, and the three women - Ashley, Jade, and Ember - rushed in, their expressions a mix of surprise and concern.

"What happened?" Ashley demanded, her gaze sweeping the room.

Samantha swallowed hard, her palms suddenly clammy. "I-I'm sorry, I didn't mean to..." she stammered, her voice trailing off.

Jade stepped forward, her emerald eyes narrowed. "How much did you hear?"

Samantha felt a surge of panic, but she forced herself to meet the woman's intense gaze. "I...I heard you talking about me. About how I might be dangerous."

Ember let out a low, frustrated growl. "I knew we shouldn't have brought her here."

Ashley raised a hand, silencing the redhead. "Calm down, Ember. This was bound to happen eventually."

She turned her attention back to Samantha, her expression unreadable. "Since you've overheard our conversation, I suppose there's no point in hiding the truth from you any longer."

Samantha swallowed hard, bracing herself for what was to come. "The truth?"

Ashley nodded, a small, enigmatic smile playing on her lips. "Yes, my dear. The truth about us..."

Trixie suddenly appeared in the doorway, her violet eyes filled with a strange mix of concern and determination. "Girls, what's going on?"

Ashley glanced over her shoulder, her gaze meeting Trixie's. "Our guest has overheard our little...discussion."

Trixie's expression darkened, and she stepped into the room, closing the door behind her. "Very well. Samantha, my dear, what you need to understand is that we are not your average group of friends."

Samantha felt her heart skip a beat, a growing sense of unease settling in the pit of her stomach. "What are you saying?"

Ashley stepped forward, her piercing gaze locking with Samantha's. "We are sorceresses."

Samantha felt the blood drain from her face, her mind racing. Sorceresses? "I...I don't understand."

Trixie moved to Samantha's side, placing a comforting hand on her shoulder. "That's why we're here, my dear. We're going to help you recover your memory."

Samantha stared at the four women, her mind reeling. Magic, sorcery, witchcraft - it was all so foreign and unbelievable. And yet, the way they spoke, the conviction in their voices, it was clear they believed every word.

"I..." Samantha began, her voice barely above a whisper. "I don't know what to say."

Ashley stepped forward, her expression softening ever so slightly. "You don't have to say anything, my dear. Just know that we are here for you, and that we will do whatever it takes to help you find yourself again."

Trixie gave Samantha's shoulder a gentle squeeze. "My dear, we never did ask - what is your name?"

Samantha hesitated, her brow furrowing. "I...I'm not sure. I don't remember anything about my past or who I am."

Ashley's gaze narrowed slightly. She turned to Trixie. "Did you happen to find anything on her when you found her, Trixie? Any identification or belongings that could give us a clue?"

Trixie pursed her lips, thinking. "Now that you mention it, I did find a wallet on her when I pulled her from the wreckage. Let me go retrieve it."

Trixie slipped out of the room, leaving the four women in tense silence. Samantha fidgeted nervously, unsure of what they might find. After a moment, Trixie returned, holding a small, leather wallet.

"Here we are," she said, handing it to Ashley. "Let's see what we can find."

Ashley carefully opened the wallet, her elegant fingers rifling through the contents. Samantha held her breath as Ashley pulled out a driver's license, her eyes scanning the information.

"Samantha," Ashley murmured, her gaze flicking up to meet Samantha's. "Your name is Samantha."

Samantha felt a strange sense of relief wash over her. At least she now had a name, even if she couldn't remember anything else about herself.

"Samantha," she repeated, testing the name on her lips. "It's nice to finally have a name, even if I don't know the rest of my story."

Jade offered her a sympathetic smile. "Don't worry, Samantha. We're going to help you uncover the truth about your past. And in the meantime, you're safe here with us."

Ember crossed her arms, her expression still somewhat sceptical. "Well, Samantha, welcome to our humble abode."

Samantha glanced around at the four women. She may not know who she was, but she was determined to find out. "I'm ready," she said, her voice steady. "Whatever it takes, I want to know the truth."

"Great!" Trixie beamed. "And then, you can become one of us!"

Ember blinked, darting her head towards them. "Wait—What? Join us? As in become one of us? No. We don't know a thing about her! Unacceptable!"

Ashley agreed, her expression turning serious. " We need to discuss this further."

Jade nodded, her brow furrowed in concern. "Yes, are you sure it's wise to bring her into our coven so quickly? We know nothing about her, and she has no memory of her past."

Ember stepped forward, her fiery gaze locked on Samantha. "Exactly. What if she's not who she seems? What if she's a threat to us and our powers?"

Trixie frowned, placing herself protectively in front of Samantha. "Now, girls, let's not jump to conclusions."

Ashley's eyes narrowed. "Trixie, we can't ignore the risks. Giving access to magic without knowing what type of person they are reckless and dangerous. Training them in magic, could end up worse. Deadly."

Samantha felt her heart racing as the four women debated her fate. She wanted to believe Trixie, to trust in the kindness they had shown her, but a part of her couldn't help but wonder if they were right to be cautious.

"I understand your concerns," Trixie said, her voice firm. "But I believe Samantha has the potential to be a powerful ally. With our guidance, she could learn to harness her abilities and use them for good."

Jade shook her head, her emerald eyes filled with worry. "Trixie, you can't be serious. We can't just trust her like that, not when we know nothing about her."

Ember nodded in agreement. "Jade's right. We need to keep a close eye on her, make sure she doesn't pose a threat. Any sign of her being dangerous, and we shut this down, no exceptions."

Ashley studied Samantha, her expression unreadable. "Very well. We'll allow Trixie to begin her training, but with strict supervision. The slightest hint of trouble, and we'll intervene."

Trixie's face brightened, and she turned to Samantha, a warm smile on her lips. "Did you hear that? We're going to help you unlock your true potential."

Samantha nodded, her mind still reeling from the heated exchange. She wanted to believe that these women had her best interests at heart, but she couldn't shake the feeling that she was walking a dangerous path.

Chapter 5

The moment the door closed behind Ashley, Jade, and Ember, Trixie turned to Samantha, her violet eyes shining with excitement.

"Now, my dear, let's not waste any time," she said, gently guiding Samantha to the edge of the bed. "We have so much to explore, so much for you to discover."

Samantha felt a flutter of apprehension in her stomach, but she couldn't deny the sense of curiosity that was building within her. "What do you mean?"

Trixie settled down beside her, her expression eager. "Your energy, Samantha. We need to get you acquainted with the energy that runs through you."

Samantha blinked, her mind struggling to wrap around the concept. "My...energy?"

She nodded excitedly. "Everything has an energy. Rub your hands together, hard, to make friction, then hold your hands close together."

At first, she felt nothing. But then, slowly, a tingling sensation began to build, in the palms of her hands. She gasped in awe. "I...I can feel it," she breathed, her voice laced with wonder.

"That's it, Samantha!" Trixie encouraged, her eyes shining with pride. "You're a natural."

Samantha searched Trixie's face, finding nothing but sincerity and conviction in her gaze. She wanted to trust the woman, to believe that she had her best interests at heart. And the thrill of wielding magic was undeniable.

After that initial lesson, Trixie continued to work with Samantha day after day, guiding her through the process of tapping into the energy that flowed through her. At first, it was little more than faint tingles and static sparks, but as the days turned into weeks, Samantha began to feel a growing power stirring.

Trixie was an enthusiastic and patient teacher, encouraging Samantha to push her limits and explore the depths of her abilities. She was trying to teach her how to focus the energy, moulding it into tangible forms, and Samantha found herself captivated by the experience.

Yet, despite her growing proficiency, Samantha's memories remained frustratingly elusive. She would spend hours in quiet contemplation, desperate to uncover even the slightest clue about her past, but to no avail. The void in her mind remained, a gaping chasm that seemed to mock her efforts.

The Shadow Sisters, true to their word, kept a close eye on Samantha's progress, though their concerns never seemed to wane.

Jade, ever the voice of reason, would try to soothe her sister's worries. "We have to give her a chance, Ember."

Ashley, ever the pragmatist, would simply nod, her expression unreadable.

And so, the days turned into weeks, with Samantha's training progressing in secret, and the Shadow Sisters keeping a wary vigil.

One afternoon, as Samantha and Trixie were deep in their latest lesson when Samantha let out a gasp. A glowing energy ball of pure light and electricity, formed in the palm of her hand. "I did it!" she squealed, almost screaming in delight.

Suddenly, a commotion outside the door drew their attention. Seconds later, the door flew open, and Ember burst into the room, her expressions a mix of alarm and fury.

Samantha, startled by the intrusion, instinctively lashed out with her newfound powers, a crackling sphere of energy taking shape in her outstretched hands. The sister paused, her eyes widening as they beheld the display of magic.

Ember's eyes narrowed, and she pointed an accusatory finger at Samantha. "I knew it! I knew we couldn't trust her. She's been learning magic behind our backs!"

Trixie opened her mouth to protest, but Ember cut her off with a sharp gesture. "No more arguments, Trixie. I'm telling the others."

Later that afternoon, the group gathered in the large, ornate dining room for a shared lunch. Samantha sat quietly, still processing all that had happened. Trixie had spent the better part of the morning teaching her how to manipulate the energy she could feel coursing through her body, and Samantha found herself both intrigued and unnerved by the experience.

As they ate, Samantha couldn't help but notice the tension that seemed to hang in the air between Ashley, Jade, and Ember. They spoke in hushed tones, occasionally glancing in her direction.

Finally, Ashley cleared her throat, drawing everyone's attention. "So, Samantha, it's been a few weeks since Trixie found you. Have you had any luck recovering your memories?"

Samantha shifted uncomfortably in her seat, shaking her head. "No, I'm afraid not. Everything from before the accident is still a complete blank."

Jade sighed, her brow furrowing with concern. "That's not entirely unusual, you know. Sometimes it can take months for memories to fully return, especially after a traumatic event."

Ember scowled, her gaze flicking over to Trixie. "Or, they might not return at all. We can't just keep her here indefinitely, waiting for something that may never happen."

Trixie's eyes narrowed, and she set her utensils down with a clatter. "And what would you suggest, Ember? Toss her out on the street, alone and vulnerable?"

Ashley raised a hand, her expression calm but firm. "Let's not get ahead of ourselves. Samantha is welcome to stay here as long as she needs to, while we try to help her regain her memories."

Ember's jaw tightened, and she leaned forward, her fiery gaze locked on Samantha. "And what if she never remembers? What if she's not who she seems, and she's just using us for her own gain?"

Jade reached out, placing a gentle hand on Ember's arm. "Ember, please. We can't jump to conclusions. Samantha has done nothing to betray our trust."

Ember jerked her arm away, her lips curling into a sneer. "That's where you're wrong, Jade. She's already learning magic, and Trixie has been training her behind our backs."

All eyes turned to Trixie, who had the decency to look sheepish. "I...I was only trying to help her get a head start."

Ashley's expression hardened, and she fixed Trixie with a stern gaze. "We discussed this, Trixie. Samantha is to get her memory back first, to find out what kind of person she really is, before we introduce her to magic!"

Trixie opened her mouth to argue, but Ember beat her to it. "I told you we couldn't trust her! Now look at what's happened - she's been learning magic, and we have no idea what she plans to do with it."

The tension in the room was palpable, and Samantha felt a sinking feeling in the pit of her stomach. She had never meant to cause any trouble, but it was clear that her presence was a source of great unease for the Shadow Sisters.

Ashley raised a hand, silencing the heated debate. "Enough. Samantha, there will be no more magic until you get your memories back. Is that understood?"

Samantha nodded, her heart pounding in her chest. "I...I understand. I don't want to cause any problems."

Ashley's expression softened slightly. "We know, Samantha. And we'll do everything in our power to help you. But we have to be cautious, for the sake of our coven."

Ember scoffed, her arms crossed defiantly over her chest. "I still don't like it. But I guess we have no choice."

The group lapsed into an uneasy silence, the tension in the air palpable. Samantha couldn't help but feel that she was walking a very fine line, and that one wrong move could spell disaster for her and the Shadow Sisters.

The air was thick with tension as Ashley, Jade, and Ember escorted Samantha and Trixie back to the site of the accident. Samantha could feel the weight of their watchful gazes as they moved through the dimly lit city streets, the shadows seeming to press in around them.

As they approached the familiar intersection, Samantha felt a shiver of unease run down her spine. There was something about this place, a deep well of emotion that she couldn't quite place. Unbidden, her steps slowed, her gaze drawn to the cracked pavement and the faint skid marks that remained.

Trixie, sensing Samantha's discomfort, reached out and gave her hand a gentle squeeze. "It's alright, my dear. We're here to help you."

Samantha nodded, though the knot of anxiety in her stomach only seemed to tighten. She couldn't shake the feeling that something important was about to happen.

Suddenly, a voice called out from across the street, causing Samantha to flinch.

"Samantha? Is that you?"

She whirled around, her eyes widening as they landed on a familiar figure. It was Maggie, her best friend, her expression a mix of shock and relief.

"Maggie?" Samantha breathed, her voice barely above a whisper.

Before she could say another word, another voice reached her ears, this one laced with a mixture of guilt and trepidation.

"Samantha? Oh, my god, you're alive."

Samantha's head snapped in the direction of the voice, and her heart plummeted as she recognized the face of her ex-boyfriend, Greg.

Suddenly, it was as if a floodgate had opened, and a torrent of memories came rushing back. The anniversary dinner, the betrayal, the heartbreak – it all came crashing down on her, and Samantha felt as if she were drowning in a sea of emotion.

But instead of the overwhelming despair she had felt that night, a new, unfamiliar sensation began to take hold – a burning, all-consuming rage.

"You," Samantha growled, her voice low and dangerous. "You bastards."

Maggie and Greg recoiled, their faces etched with fear and regret. "Samantha, we – we thought you were dead," Maggie stammered.

Samantha's lips curled into a twisted, humourless smile. "Dead? Oh, no, my dear Maggie. I'm very much alive. And now, I remember *everything*."

Chapter 6

Samantha's head pounded as the memories came flooding back. The betrayal, the anger - it all hit her like a tidal wave crashing against the shores of her mind. Her two-timing boyfriend and her best friend, sleeping together behind her back. The fight that followed, the blow to her head that landed her in the hospital. And now, the dark magic coursing through her veins, amplifying every raw emotion.

She gripped the smooth wooden staff in her hand, feeling its power hum beneath her fingertips. Trixie stood by her side, a malicious grin stretching across her face. "Time to make them pay," the dark-haired sorceress purred.

Samantha's gaze locked onto her boyfriend and best friend, who were staring back at her with a mixture of fear and guilt. "How could you?" she spat, her voice laced with venom. "All this time, right under my nose."

Her boyfriend, Ethan, took a tentative step forward. "Sam, please, it's not what you think—"

"Save it!" she snapped, swinging the staff in his direction. A bolt of energy crackled from the tip, narrowly missing him as he dove to the side.

Maggie, her treacherous best friend, threw her hands up defensively. "Samantha, we never meant to hurt you. It just… happened."

Samantha's jaw tightened. "Bullshit. You knew how much he meant to me. How could you do this?"

Trixie chuckled darkly. "Oh, the drama. I love it." She raised her staff, the obsidian gem at the top glowing with arcane power. "Let's put an end to this little love triangle, shall we?"

Before she could unleash her attack, the other two shadow sisters - Ember and Jade - stepped forward, their staves at the ready. "Trixie, stand down," Ember commanded. "This has gone too far."

Trixie scoffed. "Too far? We're just getting started." She thrust her staff forward, a swirling vortex of energy bursting forth.

Jade quickly erected a shimmering barrier, deflecting the attack. "Samantha, please, you need to calm down. We can work this out."

Samantha felt the anger coursing through her, fuelling the magic that danced across the surface of the staff. "Calm down?" she spat. "After what they did to me?" With a flick of her wrist, she sent a volley of energy blasts raining down on Ethan and Maggie.

Ember and Jade scrambled to shield the pair, their staves weaving intricate patterns in the air. "Samantha, this isn't the answer! They're our friends!"

Trixie cackled. "Friends? Ha! They betrayed her trust. They deserve whatever's coming to them."

Samantha's eyes narrowed as she watched Ethan and Maggie cower behind the sisters' protective barrier. The betrayal felt like a knife twisting in her heart. "They're not my friends. Not anymore." She poured more of her magic into the staff, feeling it respond to her rage.

Ember's brow furrowed with concern. "Samantha, listen to me. You're letting the darkness consume you. This isn't who you are."

Samantha hesitated, the weight of Ember's words causing a flicker of doubt to surface. But then the image of her boyfriend and best friend wrapped in each other's arms flashed in her mind, and the anger roared back to life. "You have no idea who I am," she snarled.

Ember's brow furrowed with concern. "Samantha, listen to me. You're letting the darkness consume you. This isn't who you are."

Samantha hesitated, the weight of Ember's words causing a flicker of doubt to surface. But then the image of her boyfriend and best friend wrapped in each other's arms flashed in her mind, and the anger roared back to life.

With a sweeping motion of the staff, Samantha tore open a shimmering portal. "Trixie, we're leaving. And you two..." She turned her glare on Ethan and Maggie. "Consider this your last chance. Stay out of my way, or I won't be so merciful next time."

Trixie cackled with delight, darting through the portal. Samantha made to follow, but Ember and Jade moved to block her path.

"We can't let you leave," Jade said, her voice firm. "Not like this."

Samantha's eyes narrowed. "Get out of my way." She swung the staff in a wide arc, unleashing a barrage of energy blasts.

Ember and Jade quickly erected a shimmering barrier, deflecting the attacks. "Samantha, please, you need to calm down. We can help you," Ember pleaded.

Samantha scoffed. "Help me? You have no idea what I'm going through." She poured more of her magic into the staff, feeling it crackle with power. "And I'm done wasting my time with you."

With a flick of her wrist, Samantha sent a volley of projectiles hurtling towards the sisters. Ember and Jade were forced to divert their attention, their barrier flickering as they struggled to keep up with the onslaught.

Ethan and Maggie cowered behind the sisters, their faces etched with terror. Samantha's gaze landed on them, and she felt a surge of rage. "This is all your fault!" she screamed, redoubling her attacks.

Ember and Jade were being pushed to their limits, their staves weaving intricate patterns as they desperately tried to shield themselves and their friends.

"Samantha, stop this!" Jade cried, her voice strained with the effort of maintaining the barrier. "You're only hurting yourself!"

But Samantha refused to listen, her mind consumed by the pain of betrayal. She poured every ounce of her anger and anguish into her assault, the air crackling with the intensity of the magic.

Suddenly, the barrier faltered, and a blast of energy slipped through, slamming into Jade's shoulder. She cried out in pain, her staff clattering to the ground as she crumpled.

Ember's eyes widened in horror. "Jade!" She turned to Samantha, her expression a mix of fear and determination. "That's enough! If you won't listen to reason, then we'll have to stop you by force."

Samantha felt a surge of triumph at the sight of Jade's injury, but a small part of her recoiled at the thought of harming her friends. Before she could act, however, Ember raised her staff, the gem at the tip glowing with a blinding light.

"Forgive me, Samantha," Ember said and then unleashed a powerful blast of energy.

Samantha tried to block the attack, but the sheer force of it sent her reeling, the staff slipping from her grasp. She crashed to the ground, her head spinning, as Ember and Jade rushed to tend to the injured Jade.

Dazed and disoriented, Samantha watched helplessly as the portal began to close, Trixie's mocking laughter echoing in her ears. "No!" she cried, struggling to her feet, but the portal snapped shut before she could reach it.

Samantha let out a scream of frustration and anguish, the magic within her swirling and pulsing with her emotions. She turned to Ember and Jade, her eyes burning with rage.

"This isn't over," she growled, her voice laced with a dark promise. "I'll make you all pay for what you've done."

Ember met her gaze with a mixture of pity and determination. "We're not giving up on you, Samantha. We'll find a way to bring you back, no matter what."

Samantha let out a bitter laugh. "Good luck with that." She glanced at Ethan and Maggie, who were watching her with a mix of fear and guilt.

With that, Samantha turned and stalked away, her mind already racing with plans for her vengeance. The darkness within her had taken hold, and she was determined to see it through, no matter the cost.

With a sweeping motion of the staff, Samantha tore open a shimmering portal. "Trixie, we're leaving. And you two..." She glared at Ethan and Maggie. "Consider this your last chance. Stay out of my way, or I won't be so merciful next time."

Trixie cackled with delight, darting through the portal. Samantha took one last look at the cowering pair, then followed, the portal snapping shut behind her.

The world on the other side was a kaleidoscope of shifting colours and bizarre, otherworldly landscapes. Samantha felt a strange sense of exhilaration as she stepped into the unknown, Trixie by her side.

"Where are we?" Samantha asked, her eyes drinking in the surreal sights around them.

Trixie's grin widened. "The Nepal. A place where the normal rules of reality don't apply. A place where we can use our magic to its full potential."

Samantha tightened her grip on the staff, feeling its power hum in response. "Good. Because I have some payback to dish out."

Trixie chuckled. "That's what I like to hear. But first, we need to make sure our dear friends can't follow us." She raised her staff, the gem at the tip glowing with a deep, violet light.

Samantha watched as Trixie wove a complex series of arcane sigils in the air, weaving a shimmering barrier around the portal. "There. That should keep them out." Trixie turned to Samantha, her eyes glinting with mischief. "Now, where shall we begin?"

Samantha's mind raced as she considered her options. The temptation to hunt down Ethan and Maggie and make them pay for their betrayal was overwhelming. But a part of her, a small, rational voice, whispered that this wasn't the answer. That giving in to the darkness would only lead to more pain.

Trixie must have sensed her hesitation because she laid a hand on Samantha's shoulder. "Don't overthink it, darling. This is your chance to take back what's rightfully yours. To show them the consequences of their actions."

Samantha's jaw tightened. "You're right. They deserve to pay." She raised her staff, feeling the power coursing through her. "Let's start with something simple. Something to send a message."

Trixie's eyes gleamed with anticipation. "I'm listening."

Samantha and Trixie materialized in a sprawling, twisted city, the very air tinged with an oppressive, otherworldly energy.

"Where are we?" Samantha asked, her gaze sweeping across the alien landscape.

Trixie gestured expansively. "Welcome to Kathmandu, the heart of the Nepal. This is where the true power lies."

Samantha could feel the magic coursing through her veins, stronger and more intense than anything she had ever experienced. "What do we do now?"

Trixie's smile was positively predatory. "Now, we have some fun." She raised her staff, the gem at the tip glowing with a sinister light. "Let's start by giving your dear friends a little… housewarming gift."

Samantha watched as Trixie unleashed a torrent of dark energy, the magic rippling through the air like a physical force. She could sense the power building, a sense of foreboding that set her teeth on edge.

Suddenly, a massive explosion rocked the city, the shockwave reverberating through Nepal. Samantha's eyes widened as she witnessed the destruction – buildings crumbling, the ground trembling, a plume of smoke and debris billowing into the sky.

"What did you do?" she asked, her voice tinged with a mix of awe and horror.

Trixie's grin was positively feral. "Just a little demonstration of our power. A taste of what's to come for your traitorous friends."

Samantha stared at the smouldering ruins, a part of her recoiling at the sheer scale of the destruction. But another part, the part that was still reeling from the betrayal, revelled in the sight. "They deserved it," she muttered, her grip tightening on the staff.

Trixie laid a hand on her shoulder, her touch almost possessive. "Of course they did, my dear. And this is only the beginning. With our combined power, we can make them pay for what they've done. We can make them all pay."

Samantha felt a chill run down her spine at the malevolent promise in Trixie's words. But even as a part of her hesitated, the memory of Ethan and Maggie's embrace burned in her mind, fuelling the rage that had taken root in her heart.

"Then let's not waste any more time," she said, her voice hard and unyielding. "Where do we start?"

Trixie's laughter echoed through the twisted streets of Kathmandu, a harbinger of the chaos and destruction that was to come.

Chapter 7

Samantha's gaze swept across the twisted, alien landscape, a mixture of awe and trepidation stirring within her. "What is this place?"

Trixie grinned, her eyes gleaming with mischief. "This is where the true power lies, Samantha. A place where we can embrace the darkness and use it to our advantage."

She gestured towards a towering spire in the distance, its obsidian façade casting an ominous shadow over the surrounding area. "That is the Raven Coven, the most powerful cabal of dark sorcerers in Nepal. They can teach you things you never imagined possible."

Samantha felt a shiver of anticipation run down her spine. The thought of harnessing such immense power was both thrilling and terrifying. "And they'll help us? Help me?" she asked, her grip tightening on the staff.

"Of course," Trixie purred. "After all, we share a common goal - making those who've wronged us pay for their betrayal." She laid a hand on Samantha's arm, her touch almost possessive. "Together, we can exact the revenge you so rightfully deserve."

Samantha hesitated, a flicker of doubt still lingering in the back of her mind. But the memory of Ethan and Maggie's embrace, the pain of their betrayal, was too fresh, too raw to ignore. With a steely resolve, she nodded. "Then let's not waste any more time."

Trixie's grin widened, and she led the way towards the imposing spire of the Raven Coven. As they approached,

Samantha could feel the air grow heavier, the very atmosphere charged with an unnatural energy.

The doors to the coven parted, and a group of robed figures emerged, their faces shrouded in darkness. Trixie bowed respectfully, and Samantha followed suit, her heart pounding with a mixture of trepidation and anticipation.

"Greetings, sisters," Trixie said, her voice laced with reverence. "I bring you a kindred spirit, one who has been wronged and seeks the power to right that wrong."

The figures regarded Samantha with an unsettling silence, their eyes glinting with a malevolent light. Finally, one of them stepped forward, her cloak parting to reveal a face that was both beautiful and terrifying.

"Welcome, child," the woman said, her voice smooth and hypnotic. "We have been expecting you."

She extended a pale, slender hand towards Samantha. "I am Malory, the High Priestess of the Raven Coven. We have heard of your plight, and we would be honoured to share our knowledge with you."

Samantha felt a strange pull towards the woman as if she were being drawn in by her very presence. "What do you require of me?" she asked, her voice barely above a whisper.

Malory's lips curled into a sinister smile. "Only your willingness to learn, and your commitment to the cause. In return, we will teach you the ways of the dark arts, and help you achieve the vengeance you so rightfully desire."

Samantha glanced back at Trixie, who was nodding encouragingly. With a deep breath, she turned to Malory and placed her hand in the High Priestess's grasp.

"I'm ready," she said, her voice steadier than she had expected.

Malory's grip tightened, and Samantha felt a surge of power coursing through her veins. "Excellent," the High Priestess purred. "Then let us begin."

As Samantha was ushered into the Raven Coven, the world around them began to change. The vibrant flowers that had dotted the landscape transformed into poisonous ivy, their vines snaking across the ground. The lush trees shed their leaves, their once-verdant branches now bare and twisted.

Samantha watched in fascination as the Raven Coven unleashed their dark magic, the very fabric of reality warping to their will. It was a display of power unlike anything she had ever seen, and a part of her thrilled at the prospect of wielding such incredible forces.

But as she followed Malory and the other coven members deeper into the spire, a small, nagging voice in the back of her mind whispered a warning. Was she truly ready to embrace the darkness, to surrender herself to the allure of vengeance?

The interior of the Raven Coven's spire was a maze of shadowy corridors and cavernous chambers, the air thick with the scent of ancient sorcery. Samantha followed Malory, her heart pounding with a mixture of trepidation and anticipation.

Finally, they entered a vast, circular chamber, the walls adorned with intricate carvings and glowing runes. In the centre stood a massive obsidian altar, its surface gleaming in the dim, flickering light.

Malory turned to face Samantha, her eyes glinting with a dangerous light. "Welcome to the heart of the Raven Coven," she said, her voice smooth and hypnotic. "This is where we harness the power of the darkness, where we bend the very fabric of reality to our will."

Samantha's grip tightened on her staff, the smooth wood thrumming with an energy that seemed to call to her. "What do I need to do?"

Malory's lips curled into a sinister smile. "First, you must learn to open yourself to the darkness, to embrace the raw, primal power that flows through all things."

She gestured towards the altar, where several ornate daggers lay in a semicircle. "Take one of those blades, child, and let the darkness flow through you."

Hesitantly, Samantha approached the altar and selected one of the daggers, its obsidian blade gleaming ominously. As her fingers wrapped around the hilt, she felt a jolt of energy course through her, like a raw, electric current.

"Good," Malory purred. "Now, close your eyes and focus. Feel the darkness within you, let it fill every fibre of your being."

Samantha did as instructed, shutting out the world around her and turning her attention inward. At first, she felt nothing, just the steady rhythm of her own heartbeat. But then, a shadow stirred deep within her, a primal, animalistic energy that sent a shiver down her spine.

"Yes, that's it," Malory's voice echoed, as if from a great distance. "Embrace the darkness, let it guide your actions."

Samantha delved deeper, allowing the darkness to flow through her, to become one with her very essence. She could feel it pulsing in her veins, whispering seductive promises of power and retribution.

Suddenly, her eyes snapped open, and she knew exactly what to do. With a fluid motion, she raised the dagger and slashed it through the air, unleashing a wave of dark energy that rippled across the chamber.

The other coven members watched in silent awe as the energy crackled and danced, twisting and reshaping the very fabric of reality. Samantha's breath caught in her throat, a thrill of exhilaration coursing through her.

Malory's laughter rang out, rich and triumphant. "Excellent, child. You have taken the first step towards unlocking your true potential."

Samantha stared at the dagger in her hand, feeling a strange sense of power and control. This was only the beginning, she realized. With the Raven Coven's guidance, she would be able to harness the darkness to her advantage, to make those who had betrayed her pay the ultimate price.

A malevolent grin spread across her face as she readied herself for the next lesson, her thirst for vengeance growing with each passing moment.

After Samantha's impressive display of dark magic, Malory regarded her with a satisfied smile. "You have shown great potential, child. With proper guidance, you will become a true master of the dark arts."

Samantha felt a surge of pride, the thrill of wielding such power still coursing through her veins. "What's next?" she asked, eager to learn more.

Malory gestured towards the other coven members, who had been observing the proceedings with silent reverence. "In three days, the moon will be full. This is a time of great power for us when the veil between our world and the mortal realm grows thin."

She stepped closer to Samantha, her eyes gleaming with a dangerous light. "During the full moon, our magic will be amplified tenfold. With your natural affinity for the darkness, the power you will wield will be unprecedented."

Samantha's breath caught in her throat, her mind racing with the implications. "What does that mean, exactly?"

Malory's lips curled into a sinister smile. "It means, my dear, that the time for retribution is at hand. With our combined strength, we will be able to reach far beyond the confines of this realm and strike at those who have wronged you."

The other coven members murmured in agreement, their voices laced with a dark anticipation.

Samantha felt a thrill of excitement, but also a twinge of apprehension. "My boyfriend and... my best friend," she said, the words tasting like bile on her tongue. "They will pay for what they've done?"

Malory nodded, her expression grave. "Indeed. They, and all those who stand in our way, will know the true meaning of pain. The world will tremble before the might of the Raven Coven, and you will have your vengeance."

Samantha closed her eyes, allowing the weight of Malory's words to sink in. Part of her recoiled at the thought of the destruction they would unleash, but the memory of Ethan and Maggie's betrayal was still too fresh, the wound too raw.

"Then let's do it," she said, her voice laced with a newfound determination. "I'm ready."

Malory's smile widened, and she placed a hand on Samantha's shoulder. "Excellent. Together, we will show the world the true power of the darkness."

The other coven members erupted into a chorus of dark chanting, their voices echoing through the chamber and sending a shiver down Samantha's spine. As she stood there, surrounded by the acolytes of the Raven Coven, she knew that there was no turning back.

The world would soon bow before them, and her ex-boyfriend and best friend would learn the true meaning of her wrath.

Chapter 8

Ember paced the small living room, her brow furrowed with worry. Jade sat on the couch, her injured shoulder wrapped in bandages, while Maggie and Ethan watched on, their faces etched with fear and guilt.

"We have to do something," Ember said, her voice tinged with urgency. "Samantha has fallen under Trixie's influence, and we have to find a way to bring her back before it's too late."

Jade winced as she tried to shift her position. "But how? Trixie's magic is powerful, and Samantha is completely consumed by her rage and thirst for vengeance."

Maggie wrapped her arms around herself, her eyes glistening with tears. "It's all my fault... if only we hadn't—"

Ethan placed a comforting hand on her shoulder, but Ember held up a hand, silencing them both.

"Placing blame won't help us now," she said firmly. "We need to focus on finding a way to break through to Samantha, to remind her of who she truly is."

The room fell silent for a moment, the weight of the situation hanging heavy in the air. Suddenly, a soft hooting sound drew their attention to the window, where a small owl perched on the sill, a rolled-up parchment tied to its leg.

Ember stepped forward cautiously, untying the message and unrolling it. Her eyes widened as she scanned the contents.

"What is it?" Jade asked, her voice strained.

"It's a warning," Ember replied, her gaze meeting Jade's. "Samantha and Trixie have been seen with the Raven Coven, speaking to their High Priestess, Malory."

Maggie's eyes widened in horror. "Malory? But she's—"

"Incredibly powerful and dangerous," Jade finished, her face pale. "If they've aligned themselves with her, we're in serious trouble."

Ethan ran a hand through his hair, his expression one of disbelief. "So, what do we do? How do we stop them?"

Ember's jaw tightened with determination. "We need to find a way to break through Trixie's barrier and get to Samantha before it's too late. And we need to find a way to strip them of their power, to keep them from causing any more destruction."

Jade nodded, wincing as the movement jostled her injured shoulder. "I may have an idea, but it will be risky. We'll need to act quickly before the full moon amplifies their magic even further."

Ember placed a reassuring hand on Jade's shoulder. "Whatever it takes, we have to try. Samantha is our friend, and we can't give up on her, no matter how far she's fallen."

The four of them huddled together, formulating a plan to save their friend and stop the Raven Coven's dark machinations. The stakes had never been higher, but they were determined to do whatever it took to bring Samantha back from the brink of darkness.

Jade turned her attention to Ethan and Maggie, her expression stern. "Before we go any further, I need to know - are you two truly remorseful for what you've done?"

Maggie's face flushed with shame, and she averted her gaze. "Of course we are. We never meant to hurt Samantha, it just...happened."

Ethan cleared his throat, shifting uncomfortably. "Yeah, we feel awful about the whole thing. I mean, we messed up, big time."

Jade's eyes narrowed, and she fixed them both with a piercing stare. "But are you sorry you got together, or just that you were caught?"

Maggie's lips pressed into a thin line, and she glanced at Ethan, who had the decency to look somewhat ashamed. "I...I don't know. I feel bad about betraying Samantha's trust, but..." She trailed off, unable to finish the thought.

Ethan, on the other hand, seemed to have no such qualms. "Look, it's not like we planned this. Samantha was always so obsessed with her studies, that she barely had time for any of us. Maggie and I, we just...connected, you know?"

Ember and Jade exchanged a pointed look, and Jade scoffed. "No wonder Samantha's so pissed. You two seem more concerned with shifting the blame than actually taking responsibility for your actions."

Maggie winced, the truth of Jade's words hitting home. But Ethan just shrugged, oblivious to the red flag Maggie had spotted in his response. "What can I say? Samantha's the one who pushed us away. We were just trying to fill the void, you know?"

Jade shook her head in disgust, her attention now firmly fixed on the greater threat they faced. "Save it. Right now, we need to focus on stopping Samantha and Trixie before they do something we'll all regret."

Ember nodded in agreement. "Jade's right. the Raven Coven is an incredibly powerful and dangerous group. We need to find a way to break through their influence and get to Samantha before it's too late."

Later that night, the faint sound of raised voices drifted from the bedroom where Ethan and Maggie had retreated. Ember and Jade glanced at each other, their expressions grave.

"We should probably give them some privacy," Jade murmured, though the tension in her voice betrayed her unease.

Ember shook her head. "No, I think we need to hear this. We need to understand what we're up against."

The sisters strained to listen as the argument escalated, the muffled words becoming increasingly clear.

"I can't believe you're still trying to justify this!" Maggie's voice rang out, laced with frustration. "We betrayed Samantha's trust, and for what? A few stolen moments of passion?"

There was a pause, and then Ethan' reply, defensive and dismissive. "It's not like we planned this. It just…happened. And it was our anniversary, for God's sake. How were we supposed to know Samantha would take it so badly?"

Jade's brow furrowed, and she exchanged a pointed look with Ember. "Their anniversary? No wonder she's so devastated. That must have felt like the ultimate betrayal."

Ember nodded grimly. "Exactly. 'It just happened' might have worked if it was a one-time thing, but this was a calculated betrayal. No wonder Samantha is so enraged."

The argument in the bedroom continued, Maggie's voice growing more agitated.

"That's the problem, Ethan! We didn't think about the consequences, about how much this would hurt Samantha. We were so wrapped up in ourselves, in our own desires, that we never stopped to consider her feelings."

Ethan scoffed. "Oh, come on. Don't put this all on me. Samantha's the one who's been obsessed with her studies, who's been neglecting us. We were just trying to find a little happiness, a little connection, where we could."

Jade's eyes widened, and she shot Ember a look of disgust. "Unbelievable!"

Ember's jaw tightened. "This explains why Samantha was so easily swayed by Trixie's manipulations. Ethan and Maggie's betrayal has left her feeling utterly alone and betrayed."

The sisters fell silent as the argument in the bedroom continued, each of them weighing the gravity of the situation they now found themselves in. With Samantha's trust so deeply shattered, and her former friends seemingly unrepentant, the path ahead was fraught with peril.

The next morning, the tension in the small apartment was palpable. Maggie and Ethan could hardly meet each other's gaze, their faces etched with guilt and unease.

Ember and Jade sipped their tea, their brows furrowed as they quietly discussed their options.

"We need to find a way to deactivate the magic in that staff, but I'm not sure we can do it without getting too close," Jade murmured, her gaze fixed on the floor.

Ember hummed in agreement. "A boomerang spell, maybe? That way, the magic would only hurt Samantha herself if she tried to use it against us."

Jade winced. "That seems a bit harsh, don't you think? We don't want to kill her, just stop her from causing any more destruction."

Ember nodded, drumming her fingers against the tabletop. "You're right. We need to find a way to safely disarm her, without risking serious harm."

Suddenly, Maggie stepped forward, her expression resolute. "I'll do it."

Ethan reached out, grasping her arm. "Maggie, no. It's too dangerous."

Maggie shrugged off his grip, her eyes hardening. "I have to try, Ethan. I owe Samantha that much, at least."

Ember and Jade exchanged a wary glance, but Ember gestured for Maggie to continue.

"Okay, what's your plan?"

Maggie took a deep breath. "I'll get close to Samantha, close enough to break the staff myself. Maybe that will be enough to disrupt the magic."

Jade shook her head. "I don't know, Maggie. Snapping the staff alone may not be enough. We need to find a way to break the orb at the top, too. That's where the real power is stored."

Maggie's brow furrowed in concentration. "Then I'll do that, too. I'll get close enough to Samantha to shatter the orb, and then maybe the magic will just... leave the staff, making it useless."

Ember regarded Maggie with a mixture of concern and admiration. "Are you sure you're up for this? Samantha is incredibly powerful now, and Trixie will be by her side. We can't guarantee your safety."

Maggie's gaze was unwavering. "I have to try. I need to make things right, for Samantha's sake. She deserves that much."

Ethan looked on, his expression a mix of worry and helplessness. "Maggie, please. There has to be another way."

Maggie turned to him, her eyes softening ever so slightly. "There isn't, Ethan. This is the only way I can think of to stop Samantha without hurting her. I have to at least try."

Ember placed a comforting hand on Maggie's shoulder. "Alright, we'll support you. But we'll be right there, ready to intervene if things get too dangerous. Understand?"

Maggie nodded, a small, determined smile tugging at the corners of her lips. "Understood. Let's do this."

The sisters exchanged a solemn look, knowing that the path ahead would be perilous. But with Maggie's bravery and their unwavering determination, they were prepared to face whatever challenges lay in wait.

Chapter 9

Trixie and the members of the Raven Coven gathered in the dimly lit council chamber, their voices hushed but filled with a palpable sense of excitement.

"The girl's power is remarkable," Malory, the High Priestess, murmured, her piercing gaze fixed on Trixie. "With her talents combined with ours, the spells we could weave would be beyond even our wildest dreams."

Trixie's lips curled into a triumphant smile. "I told you she would be the key to unlocking our true potential."

Malory arched a perfectly sculpted eyebrow, her expression one of cool calculation. "Are you so certain? Even the most jaded souls can be swayed by the pull of sentiment and morality."

Trixie waved a dismissive hand. "Please, Malory. Samantha has been betrayed by those closest to her. The darkness has already taken root – all we need to do is nurture it."

The other coven members nodded in agreement, their eyes gleaming with anticipation.

Malory's gaze narrowed as she considered Trixie's words. "That may be true, but we cannot afford any missteps. The power we could wield with Samantha's abilities would be unimaginable, but we must ensure her loyalty is absolute."

Trixie leaned forward, her eyes alight with determination. "I assure you, Malory, Samantha's loyalty is already ours. Once we show her the full extent of our power, she'll have no choice but to join us."

Malory drummed her fingers against the arms of her ornate chair, her expression thoughtful. "Even so, we cannot take any chances. The initiation ceremony on the night of the full moon must be handled with the utmost care. We need to ensure that Samantha's power is bound to ours, permanently."

Trixie nodded eagerly. "Of course, Malory. I'll make certain that Samantha is ready. She'll be ours, body and soul, by the time the moon reaches its zenith."

Malory considered Trixie's words for a long moment, her gaze drifting towards the closed door at the end of the hall, where Samantha slept. "Very well. Proceed with the preparations. But be warned, Trixie – if there are any… complications, the consequences will be dire."

Trixie's smile widened, a predatory gleam in her eyes. "Excellent. I'll make sure Samantha is ready. Once she sees the full extent of our power, she'll have no choice but to join us, body and soul."

The coven erupted into a chorus of dark laughter, the air crackling with the energy of their excitement. Malory raised a hand, silencing them.

"See that it is done. The fate of this world hangs in the balance, and we cannot afford any… complications."

Trixie nodded, already turning towards the door. "Don't worry, Malory. Her conscience won't be a problem; Samantha trusts me implicitly. I've got it all under control."

*

Samantha's eyes fluttered open, the morning light spilling through the ornate window, casting soft patterns on the floor. Her heart ached with lingering hurt, a reminder of the turmoil that had unfolded the night before. She sat up slowly, her mind clouded with confusion and anger.

The sound of boiling water filled the air, and as she took a deep breath, the soothing aroma of tea wafted toward her. Trixie entered the room, a warm smile gracing her lips as she held a steaming cup.

"Good morning, Samantha," Trixie said, her voice gentle. "I thought you could use some tea."

"Thanks," Samantha murmured, accepting the cup with trembling hands. She took a sip, the warmth spreading through her, but it did little to ease the chill in her heart.

Trixie settled beside her on the bed, her expression shifting to one of concern. "I know things feel heavy right now. But we need to prepare for what's coming."

"What do you mean?" Samantha asked, her brow furrowing.

"The Shadow Sisters," Trixie began, her tone serious. "They're plotting. They see your potential, but they also see you as a threat. We need to train. To defend ourselves."

Samantha swallowed hard, the weight of Trixie's words sinking in. "Train? But why would they—"

"Because they're afraid," Trixie interrupted, her voice sharp. "They were quick to punish you for your outburst, without even considering the pain you were in. They jumped to conclusions instead of reaching out. That's not what true friends should do. It's yet another betrayal."

Samantha felt a knot tighten in her stomach. Trixie's words echoed her own doubts. The Shadow Sisters had acted hastily, and their lack of understanding stung more than she cared to admit.

"Why do you care so much?" Samantha asked, her voice barely above a whisper. "Why are you on my side?"

Trixie laid a comforting hand on Samantha's shoulder. "Because I see the strength in you. You have a fire that they're afraid of. And fire can either burn or illuminate. I want to help you harness that power."

Samantha looked into Trixie's violet eyes, searching for sincerity. "I don't want to hurt anyone," she said, her resolve softening. "But I don't know how to control this."

"We'll figure it out together," Trixie assured her, rising to her feet. "But you need to be ready. They'll watch you closely, waiting for any sign of weakness. We can't let them take your magic away."

With a deep breath, Samantha set her cup down, determination rising within her. "Okay. I'm ready to train."

Trixie's smile returned, a glimmer of hope shining through the shadows. "Good. Let's go find the others."

As they walked down the dimly lit hall, Samantha felt a mix of anxiety and anticipation.

The air crackled with tension as Samantha stepped into the expansive training room, a cavernous space adorned with flickering candles and ancient sigils etched into the stone walls. The atmosphere buzzed with energy, a palpable reminder of the power that lay just beneath the surface.

Alyx stood at the centre of the room, her presence commanding. "Welcome, Samantha. Today, we'll begin your training in the art of defensive dark magic. It's crucial that you learn to protect yourself."

Samantha swallowed hard, her heart racing. "What do I need to do?"

"First, we'll start with a simple spell," Alyx explained, gesturing for Samantha to join her. "This technique will help you weaken any incoming attack. Think of it as draining the energy from the spell itself."

Samantha nodded, trying to focus her mind. Alyx placed her hands together, the air shimmering around her fingers. "Visualize the energy of the attack. Picture it as a wave crashing toward you. Your job is to absorb that energy, weakening it before it reaches you."

With a deep breath, Samantha mirrored Alyx's stance, her palms pressed together. "How do I absorb it?"

"By channelling your own energy," Alyx instructed, her voice smooth and persuasive. "It's all about intent. When you feel the energy approaching, redirect it, allowing it to flow through you and dissipate."

Alyx conjured a small orb of energy, hurling it toward Samantha with a flick of her wrist. As it neared, Samantha felt a rush of adrenaline. Instinctively, she extended her hands, envisioning the wave as Alyx had described. She concentrated, feeling a tingling sensation as the orb collided with her palms.

With surprising ease, she siphoned the energy, watching as the orb dimmed and faded.

"Good," Alyx praised, a glint of approval in her eyes. "You've done well. Now, let's try something more powerful."

Samantha's heart raced at the prospect. "What do you mean?"

"Elemental magic," Alyx said, her tone dripping with excitement. "With your potential, you can call upon the elements to defend yourself. Imagine summoning fire or water, bending them to your will. This will not only protect you but empower you."

"But...isn't that dangerous?" Samantha asked, her voice trembling slightly.

"Only if you lack control," Alyx reassured her. "And that's why you're here. We'll guide you every step of the way. Just remember, you're not harming anyone. You're merely manipulating the very essence of nature."

With that, Alyx began to demonstrate, raising her arms as a gust of wind swirled around them, lifting her hair and sending shivers down Samantha's spine. "Feel the energy of the elements. They're alive, and they respond to your call. Just like you absorbed the previous spell, you can draw on the power of the elements."

Samantha watched in awe as Alyx summoned a flame into her palm, the fire dancing elegantly, casting shadows across the walls. "Now it's your turn. Focus on the element you feel most connected to. Summon it, and let it flow through you."

Taking a deep breath, Samantha closed her eyes and imagined the crackling heat of fire. She could almost feel it licking at her skin, urging her to embrace its power. She raised her hands, visualizing a flicker of flame igniting between her palms.

At first, nothing happened, but then a small spark flickered to life, growing stronger as she focused. The flame surged, illuminating the room with a warm glow.

"Excellent!" Alyx exclaimed, her eyes gleaming with pride. "Now, channel that energy into a defensive spell. Use it to shield yourself from an attack."

Samantha's confidence soared. She was no longer just a victim; she was a sorceress in control of her own destiny. She envisioned the flame wrapping around her like a protective cocoon, ready to absorb any threat that came her way.

As the training session continued, Samantha felt the weight of the darkness within her shift. With each spell she learned, she grew more powerful, drawing strength from the very elements she had once feared. the Raven Coven had manipulated her, guiding her toward a path of power she never knew existed.

But deep down, a nagging feeling lingered—a warning that this newfound strength could come at a cost. And as she mastered each spell, she couldn't shake the sense that the true nature of her powers was still shrouded in shadows, waiting to be revealed.

Chapter 10

Samantha stood in the centre of the candlelit chamber, gripping her staff as a surge of dark energy crackled from its orb. Her power had grown stronger each day, and now, as she focused, she felt the energy of the room pooling at her feet, swirling in response to her command.

With a deep breath, she raised her staff, visualizing the orb growing, filling with energy that pulsed and shimmered within it. The orb flickered, then expanded, doubling in size as threads of magic coiled inside. She watched, entranced, as the orb morphed and stretched to contain her power.

Across the chamber, Trixie observed with a glint of satisfaction, her arms folded, eyes gleaming with approval. "Excellent, Samantha. You've finally unlocked control over your own magic."

Samantha smiled, a fierce pride filling her chest. "I can feel it... it's as though the energy is an extension of me."

Trixie nodded. "Exactly. Dark magic isn't just about strength—it's about owning the power, letting it reflect your desires." She took a step forward, her gaze lingering on Samantha's staff, now radiating an eerie violet light. "You've done well expanding the orb, but I believe you're ready to channel even more."

Samantha met Trixie's gaze, her pulse quickening. "You mean... elemental magic?"

"Yes," Trixie replied, her voice a whisper of temptation. "Earth, air, fire, and water. It will amplify everything you can already do." She extended her hands, her staff lighting up in demonstration. Wisps of wind began to swirl around them, spiralling upward until the flames of the candles flickered. With a flick of her wrist, she directed the gust toward Samantha, who felt the weight of the air pressing against her.

Samantha lifted her staff, instinctively drawing from the orb's energy to counter the wind. She sent a powerful surge of magic forward, and the wind dissipated, leaving the air still and charged. Trixie gave a pleased nod. "Very good. Now, control the element on your own. Try... fire."

Taking a steadying breath, Samantha focused on the orb's core, visualizing flames. She recalled the raw anger she felt every time she thought of her past, fuelling her magic with the memories. Slowly, a spark appeared within the orb, which ignited and grew until the tip of her staff blazed.

Samantha felt the heat radiating from it, but it didn't hurt her—instead, the fire felt like part of her, a warm, pulsing extension of her will. She concentrated, pushing her power outward. The flames leapt higher, casting shadows that danced along the walls.

"See how easily it responds to you?" Trixie's voice was low, her eyes never leaving Samantha's staff. "Soon, you'll be able to summon storms, move rivers, and raise earth from the ground. You're already so close."

The words ignited something inside Samantha. She lowered the staff, her fingers brushing the now-larger orb, feeling the unbridled magic humming beneath the surface. "I want to learn it all, Trixie. Every element, every spell. I want power."

Trixie's lips curved into a satisfied smile. "And you shall have it. But remember, Samantha, this power comes with a price. The more you take, the more you become bound to it."

Samantha only nodded, the warning a mere afterthought. The thrill of power coursed through her, and she gripped her staff tightly, relishing the weight of the enhanced orb and the potential it promised.

"Then let's continue," she said, a fierce determination in her voice. "Show me everything."

Samantha met Carol's glare head-on, her grip on her staff steady. She tilted her head, a hint of a smile tugging at her lips. "Since you're so curious, let me clear something up—I remember everything. My memory returned long before I arrived here. So, whatever you think you know about me or my past, it means nothing."

The coven members exchanged looks of surprise, their whispers filling the chamber like the rustling of leaves. Carol's sneer faltered, but she recovered quickly, her eyes narrowing with contempt.

"Oh, I'm sure you're proud of that," she scoffed, glancing at her fellow coven members, "but confidence is no substitute for experience."

Behind Samantha, another witch, Carol's closest friend, murmured a few incantations under her breath. Samantha didn't see the sudden flicker of green energy streaking toward her back, but Trixie did. With a swift, fluid motion, Trixie raised her hand, intercepting the hex mid-flight. It shattered, the dark energy dissipating harmlessly in the air as Trixie's fingers curled around the spell.

A hush fell over the room as Trixie took a step forward, her eyes blazing as she looked directly at Carol's friend. "Is this how the coven treats its own? Attacking a sister from behind?"

The Sorceress' Claim

The witch shrank back, casting a wary glance at Carol, who averted her gaze, biting her lip.

Trixie turned to Samantha, her expression softening. "You may be new to the coven, Samantha, but you don't stand alone." She glanced around the room, her voice cold and unyielding. "Anyone who forgets that will answer to me."

A chill silence filled the hall, broken only by the shuffling of feet as the witches avoided Trixie's piercing gaze. Samantha felt a surge of gratitude mixed with awe. Trixie had been watching out for her all along, quietly ensuring her protection and pushing her power forward, even as others tried to undermine her.

Samantha turned back to Carol, her eyes filled with steely resolve. "I don't care what you think of me. I'm here to stay, whether you like it or not."

Carol glared at her for a moment, but finally lowered her eyes, her mouth pressed into a thin line. She knew better than to challenge Trixie again—at least, not openly.

Satisfied, Trixie gestured for Samantha to follow her out of the chamber. "Come, Samantha," she said warmly. "You've more than proven yourself. Let's focus on what matters—strengthening your power."

As they left the hall, Samantha felt her loyalty to Trixie deepens. Whatever others thought of her here, she had one true ally.

Here's the next scene, where Samantha and Trixie's lunch is interrupted by the suspicious owl. This interaction will deepen the mystery and show Trixie's strategic nature while hinting at Samantha's growing awareness.

Samantha and Trixie settled at a small wooden table outside the coven's dining hall, the crisp autumn air carrying the faint scent of sage and rosemary from the nearby gardens. Samantha's mind was still lingering on the confrontation with Carol and the other witches, but the soft clink of plates brought her back to the present. Lunch was a welcome distraction, and the warm stew on the table was a comforting reminder that not everything had to be so intense.

As they ate, Samantha felt a prickle on the back of her neck, an odd sensation she couldn't quite place. She glanced around, her gaze drifting to a gnarled old tree a few yards away. There, perched on a low branch, was a tawny owl, its unblinking gaze fixed directly on her.

She let out a short laugh, waving it off. "You know, I almost thought that owl was watching us. Just my paranoia acting up."

Trixie raised an eyebrow, turning her attention to the bird. Her eyes narrowed, and a thin, calculated smile crossed her face. Without a word, she lifted her hand, her fingers flickering with a touch of magic. A faint spark shot out, arcing toward the owl like a tiny lightning bolt.

With a startled screech, the owl fluffed its wings, hopping back before launching itself into the air. It flapped off, disappearing into the shadows of the forest canopy.

Samantha watched the display, her fork frozen mid-air. "Trixie, what was that?"

Trixie gave her a small, conspiratorial smile. "That was insurance, my dear. Witches of certain covens have a way with animals, you know. It's an old trick—one that allows them to watch others without being seen themselves."

Samantha felt a shiver run down her spine. "You think it was spying on us?"

"Could be," Trixie replied, her tone matter-of-fact. "Some witches bind animals to their magic. They'll use them to fly over places they dare not go, or to listen in on things they're not meant to hear."

The idea of a creature watching her at someone else's command sent a strange, unsettled feeling through Samantha. It was unsettling—and yet something about Trixie's easy confidence in dealing with it struck her as curious. "Is that why you're always so careful? Watching everything?"

Trixie smiled, taking a sip of her tea. "Let's just say, in our world, paranoia can be an asset. But a little caution is only natural," she said, giving Samantha a pointed look. "Especially when you have something worth protecting."

Samantha nodded, her mind spinning. She'd always thought she might be overly cautious, maybe even a little too careful. But seeing Trixie's wariness—and her quickness to ward off any threat—made her wonder. Perhaps it wasn't paranoia, but wisdom.

Still, a flicker of doubt crossed her mind. Trixie's actions were almost too precise, her suspicions always on high alert. Was this simple caution, or something deeper? Samantha wasn't sure whether she was becoming more observant or if she, too, was beginning to share Trixie's distrust.

With a glance back at the empty tree, Samantha pushed the thought away. Maybe Trixie was right: a little paranoia couldn't hurt.

Chapter 11

The forest felt colder than usual as the Shadow Sisters, along with Ethan and Maggie, made their way through the winding path to the ancient, twisted tree that marked the beginning of the Raven Coven's territory. Shadows gathered beneath its skeletal branches, twisting over the frosted ground, and a biting wind swept through, carrying with it the scent of damp earth and winter.

Jade led the way, her eyes sharp as she surveyed their surroundings, her bag of potions and talismans swinging at her side. Each step seemed to echo in the silent woods, the usual sounds of birds or small animals eerily absent, as if even the forest itself knew what they were up against.

Maggie shivered, tugging her cloak tighter around her shoulders. She glanced nervously at Ethan, who walked beside her with a determined set to his jaw, though she could tell he was just as unsettled as she was. She reached into her pocket, fingers brushing the cold metal of a protective talisman Jade had given her earlier—a charm to ward off curses. Its weight brought little comfort.

"This will work, won't it?" Maggie whispered, her voice barely audible over the wind. "These charms, the potions... everything we brought?"

Jade paused, glancing back at her with a steady gaze. "They're meant to shield you from dark magic, yes. But Samantha... she's different now. We'll need more than potions and talismans if she's truly gone down that path."

Maggie's heart clenched. The Samantha she remembered was gone, replaced by someone powerful, someone consumed by anger and darkness. She felt an icy dread creep up her spine. She clutched the talisman in her hand, wishing it could somehow strengthen her resolve. "What if she doesn't even listen to us?" she murmured. "What if... what if she kills me before I even get close enough to break her staff?"

Ethan put a reassuring hand on her shoulder, though his expression was strained. "We'll keep you safe, Maggie. Just stay close to Jade and Ember. Remember, they know what they're doing."

Jade exchanged a look with Ember, who walked beside her with a grim set to her mouth. "Ethan is right," Ember said. "We're here to protect you and make sure you have a chance to do what's needed. But you need to trust us and follow exactly what we say."

Maggie nodded, but the fear gnawed at her. What if she wasn't strong enough to confront Samantha? What if, when the moment came, she couldn't bring herself to do it?

They reached the twisted tree, its ancient, gnarled trunk seeming to loom over them like a silent guardian. Jade stopped, kneeling to set down her bag and pull out small vials and amulets, handing them to each of the group.

"Take one of these," Jade said, her voice low. "The potions will help conceal our presence from Samantha's magic, at least until we're closer. But once she senses us, be ready."

Maggie accepted the potion, her hands trembling as she held it to her lips. She could feel the weight of everyone's expectations, the cold reality of what she had to do pressing down on her. She wanted to believe that Samantha could be saved, that maybe they wouldn't have to resort to this, but the memory of Samantha's rage still burned in her mind.

She swallowed the potion in a single gulp, bracing herself for the bitter taste that lingered on her tongue. Beside her, Ethan did the same, his hand brushing against hers as if to offer a final measure of reassurance.

As the cold wind swept through the forest, whistling through the branches above, Maggie's doubts grew sharper. She could feel her resolve fraying, slipping under the weight of her fear. The forest seemed to close in, the shadows pressing down around her as if to remind her of what lay ahead.

Jade's voice cut through her spiralling thoughts. "It's time to go. We stay together, and we do this as a team. Stay close and keep moving forward."

With that, they began their approach, the tree fading into the shadows behind them as they disappeared into the depths of the forest, heading toward whatever awaited them in the darkness.

The forest seemed to close in around them as they walked, the shadows of bare branches stretching across the ground like skeletal hands. Maggie's sense of unease only grew the silence thickening with each step. She glanced sideways at Ethan, his usual air of confidence unshaken.

Ethan caught her glance, rolling his eyes slightly. "You're worried over nothing, Maggie. Samantha's not going to hurt anyone. She's just... confused. We'll talk to her, remind her who she is, and this will all blow over."

Maggie stopped in her tracks, giving him a hard look. "You think she's 'just confused'? She nearly tore apart the town square the last time she lost control. She's not exactly in a mood to listen."

Ethan sighed, waving her off. "You're overreacting. Samantha's not going to kill anyone, least of all, us. Once she sees reason, she'll snap out of it."

Maggie clenched her fists, anger bubbling up as her patience wore thin. "Why do you always dismiss everything like this? Do you really think this is just a minor argument we can 'snap out of'? We're dealing with dark magic here, Ethan, and this situation is dangerous because of people like you who can't take it seriously."

Ethan chuckled under his breath, his usual smugness intact. "I know Samantha better than you, Maggie. She's angry, sure, but she's got a good heart. She just needs a nudge in the right direction."

As his words sank in, Maggie felt her stomach twist. How many times had she ignored this side of him, brushed off his arrogance as confidence? She could see the red flags clearer than ever now—the stubbornness, the disregard for anyone else's concerns. Had Samantha put up with the same indifference, the same careless dismissal?

A realization struck her, bitter and unsettling. Had Samantha already seen all this in Ethan and chosen to look past it? Had she, Maggie, fallen into the same trap?

"Ethan," she began, her voice taut with frustration, "you can't just shrug off the damage that's been done. Stop acting like this is just some inconvenience we're going to walk away from unscathed. We're responsible for what's happened to Samantha, too. And if you can't accept that, then maybe it's time you finally own up to your part in all of this."

Before Ethan could respond, a rustling sound came from the shadows. Maggie froze, her voice hanging in the air, her heart pounding. She felt an unsettling prickle run down her spine as three figures emerged from behind a cluster of trees.

One of them stepped forward, a tall woman with sharp eyes and a cold expression. Her lips curved into a smile that was anything but friendly. "Well, well," she sneered. "What do we have here? Strangers wandering into Alyx coven territory?"

Ethan squared his shoulders, his voice losing its usual confidence as he called out, "We're just passing through. No need to make a fuss."

The woman exchanged a dark look with her companions, a cruel smile playing on her lips. "Passing through?" she echoed, her voice dripping with sarcasm. "Is that what they're calling trespassing these days?"

Maggie's pulse quickened, her fingers tightening around the protective talisman in her pocket. She tried to get a read on the strangers, but the woman's expression was cold and unyielding. Maggie could see faint glimmers of dark magic swirling at the edges of her hands, and something told her this woman wasn't one for negotiations.

Ethan, still clinging to his air of control, lifted a hand in a placating gesture. "We didn't mean any harm. We'll be on our way."

But the woman's eyes narrowed, her smile widening as her hands glowed with a dangerous energy. "Oh, I don't think so. You see, people like you aren't welcome here. And we've been humiliated enough lately—time we took it out on someone."

Before Maggie could process the threat, the woman raised her hand, releasing a stream of dark energy that streaked toward them. Maggie ducked, the spell crashing into the ground beside her, leaving a small scorch mark in the earth.

"What the hell?" Ethan shouted, his calm facade finally shattering as he scrambled to reach for his own protective charm.

The woman's companions laughed, their voices low and taunting as they moved closer, surrounding Maggie and Ethan. Maggie's heart pounded, her fear mingling with anger as she realized the gravity of their situation. They weren't just trespassers—they were targets.

Maggie took a steadying breath, her voice tight as she looked at Ethan, seeing him as if for the first time. "This is real, Ethan. And you'd better hope you're ready for the consequences."

The woman sneered, her hand lighting up again with magic, readying for another attack. Maggie could feel her resolve harden, the weight of her talisman reassuring in her hand. Whatever doubts she'd had, whatever misgivings, vanished. Now, survival was all that mattered.

Chapter 12

Carol's pulse pounded in her ears as she watched the two trespassers stumble back, their eyes wide with surprise. She recognized the look all too well—panic, fear. They hadn't expected to face anyone here, much less a group of witches ready to defend their ground. She relished it.

Her fists clenched as her thoughts returned to her humiliating defeat in front of Trixie and Samantha. She'd been made to look like a fool, stripped of her pride and mocked by a woman she'd once considered barely worthy of attention. Now, Carol's vision narrowed, her anger fuelling the magic that sparked between her fingers.

She saw the two intruders fumbling with their talismans, and a fresh wave of disdain washed over her. The way they relied on these meagre charms was pathetic. Did they really think a few trinkets would protect them from the Raven coven witches? The arrogance was laughable.

Without a second thought, she thrust her hand forward, sending a concentrated bolt of energy directly at them. Her aim was true—she struck the talismans clean from their hands, watching with grim satisfaction as the charms flew into the underbrush.

The woman's eyes widened in terror, glancing at her now-empty hands. The man, on the other hand, let out a strangled curse, his confidence shattering into panic as he took a step back, his gaze darting from Carol to his now-vulnerable companion.

Carol's lips curled into a sneer. "Look at you," she taunted. "All your bravado gone. What were you thinking, wandering into Raven territory without knowing who you were dealing with?"

The man's face paled, and Carol's satisfaction only deepened. She took a step closer, her magic thrumming at her fingertips. "Don't worry," she murmured, her voice dark and mocking. "This will be over quickly."

But then, to her surprise, the man grabbed the woman's arm, pulling her backwards. "We're getting out of here!" he hissed, his voice tight with fear. Without another word, he turned and bolted, dragging the woman along with him as they stumbled into the forest.

Cowards. Carol's jaw clenched as she watched them flee, anger simmering beneath the surface. She'd expected more from them, at least enough courage to stand and fight. But it was clear now that they'd come ill-prepared, relying on their flimsy charms and their naive belief that they could talk their way out of trouble.

The two remaining women, however, were different. Shadow Sister witches—she could see it in their hardened expressions, the way they braced themselves, their eyes glinting with defiance rather than fear. They weren't going to run, and that only made Carol's blood boil hotter. These were the types of witches who thought they were better than her, who thought their light magic gave them some kind of superiority.

Well, they would learn. They would see just how wrong they were.

Carol turned to her own companions, who were watching her with a mixture of excitement and unease. She raised her hand, signalling them forward. "No mercy," she said, her voice cold

The Sorceress' Claim

and unyielding. "These Shadow Sisters think they can just waltz into our territory? It's time we showed them what that costs."

With that, she moved forward, her magic crackling to life in her palms. The wind picked up around them, whipping through the trees as she focused on the two remaining witches, her anger sharp and unrelenting. She would make them regret every step they'd taken into Raven territory.

As she launched her next spell, she saw the fear flash in the Shadow Sisters' eyes, and it was almost enough to satisfy her. Almost. But not quite.

Not until they were broken.

The two Shadow Sisters braced themselves, eyes narrowed as Carol and her companions advanced, magic swirling around them like storm clouds gathering for a downpour. Carol smirked, relishing the fear and defiance in their eyes.

"Ready to regret trespassing?" she sneered, her voice laced with venom.

Before they could respond, Carol raised her hands, unleashing a powerful bolt of dark energy that crackled through the air, arcing toward the Shadow Sisters with deadly precision. One of them, a dark-haired witch with a steady gaze, quickly raised a shimmering shield, intercepting the bolt. The force of Carol's attack rippled through the air, pushing the witch back several feet as she gritted her teeth to hold her ground.

Carol's companions followed her lead, casting spells that split through the air like jagged lightning, slamming into the Shadow Sisters' defences. The forest was filled with bursts of colour and crackling magic as the two groups clashed, each spell more destructive than the last. Trees splintered and leaves scattered, caught in the whirlwind of energy. The Shadow Sisters fought valiantly, their light magic clashing against the darkness, but they were quickly outnumbered and overwhelmed.

Carol advanced again, her fury driving her magic to new heights. She sent another blast forward, this time breaking through the defences of the other Shadow Sister. The witch was thrown backwards, her body slamming against a tree as she let out a pained cry, blood dripping from a wound on her forehead.

The first witch lunged forward, casting a blinding light that momentarily stunned Carol and her companions. It was a desperate move, buying her and her injured companion a precious second to catch their breath.

"We're not... done yet," the injured witch gasped, struggling to her feet despite the blood trickling down her face.

Carol laughed, her voice cold and mocking. "You're done the moment you crossed into our lands."

She summoned her remaining strength, dark energy pooling in her palms as she prepared to deliver the final blow. But just as she launched her spell, the other Shadow Sister, weakened but undeterred, thrust her own magic forward, countering Carol's attack with a blast of light that exploded on impact.

The force of the explosion rocked the forest, sending Carol and the other witches stumbling backwards. Branches snapped, and dust filled the air as the shockwave rattled the trees. When the dust settled, Carol looked up, her eyes blazing as she spotted the two Shadow Sisters, bloodied and bruised, struggling to get to their feet, their breaths coming in ragged gasps.

Despite their condition, the Shadow Sisters managed to take a few shaky steps backwards, moving deeper into the forest as they clutched each other for support.

"You won't get far," Carol spat, her voice hoarse but still filled with venom.

She reached into her cloak, pulling out a small amulet. Closing her eyes, she channelled a message, her magic pulsing through the amulet as she mentally connected with Malony, one of the coven's leaders. *"Malony, it's Carol. Shadow Sisters have been spotted nearby. They're searching for Trixie and Samantha. I've dealt with them for now, but they won't be alone for long."*

Maggie paused, then Malony's voice crackled through the connection, laced with anger. *"Understood. We'll prepare for them. Don't let them slip away again."*

The connection faded, and Carol's gaze hardened as she pocketed the amulet. Her companions looked at her, their own injuries evident but their determination unwavering. She straightened, wiping the blood from her face as she prepared to pursue the fleeing Shadow Sisters.

"Let's finish what we started," she murmured, her voice steely.

The hunt was on, and this time, Carol would make sure there were no survivors.

*

Malory's brow furrowed as Carol's message crackled through the amulet, her grip tightening around the ancient artefact. The Shadow Sisters had dared to venture into their territory, and that was an offence she would not tolerate.

She swept through the dimly lit council chamber, her robes billowing behind her. The other coven members turned to face her, sensing the disturbance in the air.

"Carol has encountered the Shadow Sisters," Malory announced, her voice laced with a barely contained fury. "They are searching for Trixie and Samantha."

A murmur of discontent rippled through the room, the witches exchanging dark glances. Malory raised her hand, silencing them.

"This cannot be allowed to stand. The Shadow Sisters have meddled in our affairs for far too long." Her piercing gaze swept over the assembled coven. "Prepare the others. We will meet this threat head-on."

One of the younger witches, Nyx, stepped forward, her eyes gleaming with a mix of excitement and trepidation. "What of Samantha and Trixie? Shall we bring them into the fray?"

Malory considered the question for a moment, her expression unreadable. "No. Samantha's powers are still too unpredictable. I will not risk her losing control in the midst of battle." Her lips curled into a cold smile. "Let the Shadow Sisters contend with the full might of the Raven Coven."

The other witches nodded, their own smiles mirroring Malory's. They knew better than to question her decision – when the High Priestess spoke, they obeyed without hesitation.

As the coven members dispersed to ready themselves for the coming confrontation, Malory remained, her thoughts consumed by the gravity of the situation. The Shadow Sisters were a persistent thorn in her side, their meddling a constant annoyance. But this time, they had gone too far.

She clenched her fist, feeling the power of the Raven Coven coursing through her veins. They would not be caught off-guard this time. The Shadow Sisters would learn a harsh lesson about the consequences of trespassing on the Raven Coven's territory.

With a swirl of her robes, Malory followed the others, her mind already strategizing, plotting the best way to crush the interlopers once and for all. the Raven Coven would emerge victorious, and their enemies would be reduced to ashes.

Nothing would stand in their way, not even the Shadow Sisters and their feeble attempts to interfere.

Chapter 13

Samantha sipped her tea, the warm liquid soothing her as she sat across from Trixie in the cosy café. It had been a long, gruelling training session, and the quiet atmosphere of the establishment provided a welcome respite.

As she gazed out the window, watching the passersby, Samantha couldn't help but notice the hushed whispers and furtive glances directed their way. It seemed the news of her alliance with the Raven Coven had spread quickly through the local magical community.

Trixie, ever observant, leaned in, her violet eyes gleaming with amusement. "It appears our presence has caused quite a stir, my dear."

Samantha nodded, her brow furrowing slightly. "I don't understand. Why are they looking at us like that?"

Trixie chuckled, taking a sip of her tea. "Oh, Samantha, don't you see? They're afraid of you. Or, more accurately, they're afraid of what you've become."

Samantha felt a twinge of unease at Trixie's words. "What do you mean? I'm the same person I've always been."

Trixie shook her head, her expression turning solemn. "No, my dear, you're not. The power you've harnessed, the darkness you've embraced – it's changed you, in ways they can't begin to comprehend."

Samantha opened her mouth to protest, but Trixie raised a hand, silencing her. "Don't be alarmed. It's not a bad thing. In fact, it's a testament to your strength, and your resilience. You've become a force to be reckoned with."

Samantha considered Trixie's words, her gaze drifting back to the other patrons. Now that she really looked, she could see the fear and uncertainty in their eyes, the way they quickly averted their gaze whenever she met their stare.

"They think I'm under some kind of spell, don't they?" she murmured, realization dawning on her.

Trixie nodded, her expression sympathetic. "Yes, my dear. They simply can't fathom that you've made this choice of your own free will. To them, the Samantha they knew could never align herself with the Raven Coven."

Samantha felt a pang of frustration. "But they're wrong. I remember everything now – the betrayal, the pain. This is my choice, and I'm stronger for it."

Trixie reached across the table, giving Samantha's hand a gentle squeeze. "I know, Samantha. And soon, they'll all see it, too. But for now, we must be vigilant. There are those who will try to interfere, to take what is rightfully yours."

As if on cue, the door to the café burst open, and a group of young, determined-looking witches stormed in. Samantha recognized one of them – a girl she had known from her old coven, Lydia.

Lydia's eyes were alight with a mixture of fear and determination as she strode towards their table, the other witches trailing behind her.

"Samantha, what have you done?" Lydia cried, her voice trembling. "How could you join the Raven Coven? They're dangerous, they're—"

Trixie rose from her seat, her expression darkening. "They're what, my dear? Powerful? Uncompromising? I'm afraid you've simply fallen victim to the same narrow-minded prejudice as the others."

The young witches faltered, exchanging uncertain glances. Lydia, however, stood her ground, her chin raised defiantly.

"We can't let you get away with this, Samantha. You're not thinking clearly – they've bewitched you, corrupted you. We're here to bring you back."

Samantha felt a surge of anger rising within her. "Bewitched? Corrupted?" she spat, her grip tightening on the edge of the table. "You have no idea what I've been through, what I've lost. The Raven Coven has given me the power to fight back, to take what's rightfully mine."

Lydia's eyes widened, her resolve faltering for a moment. "But Samantha, this isn't you. You're kind, you're—"

"I'm what?" Samantha interrupted, her voice cold and hard. "Weak? Powerless? Well, that Samantha is gone. And I'm never going back."

With a flick of her wrist, Samantha unleashed a burst of dark energy, sending the young witches flying backwards. They crashed against the walls, their cries of pain and surprise echoing through the café.

Trixie watched the display with a satisfied smirk, her arms folded across her chest. "I did try to warn you, my dear."

Samantha felt a strange sense of detachment as she watched the witches struggle to their feet, their faces etched with fear and disbelief. She had once counted them as friends, but now they were nothing more than obstacles in her path.

The sound of approaching footsteps and the wail of an ambulance siren drew their attention, and Trixie placed a hand on Samantha's arm.

"I believe that's our cue to make ourselves scarce, my dear. We wouldn't want to be here when the medics arrive, now would we?"

Samantha nodded, and with a final glance at the crumpled forms of the young witches, she followed Trixie out of the café and into the waiting shadows.

As they walked, Samantha couldn't shake the lingering unease she felt. The look of betrayal and horror on Lydia's face had struck a chord within her, a faint echo of the emotions she had once felt. But she pushed those thoughts aside, reminding herself that she had chosen this path, and there was no going back.

The power of the Raven Coven coursed through her veins, and she would use it to take back what was rightfully hers. Nothing would stand in her way, not even the feeble attempts of those who still clung to the delusion of the old Samantha.

*

Later that day, Samantha found herself once again in the training room, Trixie's intense gaze fixed upon her as she worked through a series of complex spells. The burst of power she had unleashed in the café had only fuelled Trixie's determination to push her further, to extract every ounce of her potential.

"Again, Samantha," Trixie commanded, her voice sharp and unyielding. "The elemental energy must flow through you seamlessly, like an extension of your own being."

Samantha gritted her teeth, her brow furrowed in concentration as she summoned the swirling energy, weaving it into intricate patterns. Flames danced at her fingertips, twisting and swirling in response to her will. But Trixie's expression remained critical, her lips pressed into a thin line.

"Faster, Samantha. The enemy will not wait for you to catch your breath," she chided.

Samantha felt a surge of frustration, but she pushed herself harder, the flames growing brighter and hotter. She could feel the power coursing through her, the darkness within her fuelling the intensity of her spell casting.

As the training session wore on, Samantha's movements became sharper, and more precise. She could sense Trixie's approval, even if the older witch didn't outwardly express it. But despite her progress, a nagging doubt lingered in the back of her mind.

The image of the young witches, their pained expressions as they crumpled to the ground, had stirred something within her – a flicker of remorse, a hesitation that she had quickly suppressed. But Trixie had noticed it, and Samantha could see the calculating gleam in her eyes.

As they finally paused for a break, Trixie produced a small vial, its contents shimmering with a faint, purple hue.

"Samantha, my dear, I have something for you," Trixie said, her voice dripping with false sweetness.

Samantha eyed the vial suspiciously. "What is it?"

Trixie's lips curved into a smile, but there was no warmth in her expression. "Just a little something to help you stay focused, to keep that edge you've developed. Drink up."

Samantha hesitated, her gaze flicking between the vial and Trixie's face. There was something about the older witch's demeanour that unsettled her, a subtle shift in her usually comforting presence.

"Trixie, what is this?" she asked, her voice barely above a whisper.

Trixie's smile widened, and she pressed the vial into Samantha's hand. "Trust me, Samantha. This will only make you stronger, more resilient to the doubts that may still linger."

Samantha stared at the vial, her fingers trembling slightly. She knew Trixie had her best interests at heart, that she was guiding her towards true power. But something about this felt wrong, a nagging sense of unease that she couldn't quite shake.

"The fact that those witches are still alive concerns me, Samantha," Trixie continued, her voice low and conspiratorial. "It means there is still a part of you that holds back, that hesitates. And we simply can't have that, can we?"

Samantha's grip tightened on the vial, the cool glass biting into her palm. Trixie was right – she had felt that flicker of remorse, that whisper of her former self that still clung to her. And it terrified her.

"What will this do to me?" she asked, her voice barely audible.

Trixie reached out, cupping Samantha's cheek with a gentle hand. "It will free you, my dear. It will strip away the last vestiges of the old Samantha, leaving only the powerful, uncompromising sorceress you were meant to be."

Samantha stared into Trixie's eyes, searching for any sign of deception. But all she saw was unwavering conviction, a determination that both thrilled and unnerved her.

Samantha stared at the vial, her brow furrowed with suspicion. "I don't need some potion to make me stronger, Trixie. I've come this far through my own power, and that's not going to change."

Trixie's expression darkened for the briefest of moments, but she quickly schooled her features into a mask of understanding. "My dear Samantha, I only want to help you reach your full potential. That remnant of your old self is holding you back, and this potion will help you overcome it."

Samantha shook her head, firmly pushing Trixie's hand away. "No. I'm not going to let some concoction strip away who I am. I know what I want, and I don't need your tricks to get there."

Trixie's lips tightened, but she managed a placating smile. "Very well, Samantha. I won't force you. But please, at least take a break and have a sip of water. You've been working so hard, and I'd hate for you to become dehydrated."

Samantha eyed Trixie warily, but the older woman's expression was one of genuine concern. With a resigned sigh, Samantha nodded and accepted the glass of water Trixie offered.

As Samantha brought the glass to her lips, Trixie watched, her gaze carefully concealing the subtle triumph in her eyes.

Samantha took a long, refreshing sip, unaware of the insidious plot unfolding around her. The cool water felt soothing against her throat, and she let out a content sigh as she lowered the glass.

Trixie observed her with a feigned innocence. "Feeling better, my dear?"

Samantha nodded, a small smile tugging at the corners of her lips. "Yes, actually. That hit the spot."

Trixie's own lips curled into a satisfied grin. "Excellent. Now, shall we continue with your training? I have a few more exercises I'd like you to try."

As Samantha followed Trixie back to the centre of the training room, the potion began to take effect, its magic coursing through her veins. Samantha felt a strange, tingling sensation, and a sense of heightened focus and determination that she hadn't experienced before.

Trixie observed the subtle changes in Samantha's demeanour, her eyes gleaming with a mix of triumph and anticipation. The last vestiges of the old Samantha were about to be stripped away, leaving only the powerful, uncompromising sorceress that Trixie had always known Samantha could become.

With each spell Samantha cast, the potion's influence grew stronger, fuelling her magic with a dark, consuming intensity. Trixie watched, her smile widening, as Samantha's movements became sharper, more precise – and more ruthless.

The hesitation, the flicker of remorse that had once lingered, was now gone, replaced by a single-minded determination to master the dark arts. Trixie knew that the final transformation was nearly complete, and soon, Samantha would be ready to embrace her true destiny.

As the training session drew to a close, Samantha stood, her expression calm and focused. Gone was the last trace of the old Samantha, the one who had once recoiled at the thought of embracing the darkness. Now, she was a force to be reckoned with, a sorceress who would stop at nothing to achieve her goals.

Trixie placed a hand on Samantha's shoulder, her touch possessive. "Well done, my dear. I knew you had it in you."

Samantha met Trixie's gaze, her own eyes burning with an intensity that sent a shiver down the older witch's spine. "Thank you, Trixie. For everything."

Trixie's smile widened, and she knew that her gamble had paid off. Samantha was now firmly under her control, her conscience and doubts stripped away by the combined power of the potions. The old Samantha was gone, and in her place stood a formidable sorceress, one who would stop at nothing to achieve her vengeance.

Chapter 14

The days that followed were a blur of intense training and unchecked power for Samantha. With each passing hour, she could feel the darkness within her growing stronger, more consuming. The potion Trixie had secretly slipped into her water had stripped away the last vestiges of her former self, leaving her wholly committed to the pursuit of dark magic and vengeance.

Samantha's spellcasting had become a thing of raw, unrestrained fury. Where she had once hesitated, her movements now flowed with ruthless precision, the very elements bending to her will. The other coven members, even Raven and Jade, watched with a mix of awe and unease as Samantha's abilities reached new heights.

Trixie, however, revelled in Samantha's transformation. She had not only succeeded in breaking down the last of Samantha's moral reservations but had also managed to keep the potency of the potion a secret from the High Priestess, Malory.

As Samantha honed her skills, unleashing her power in increasingly destructive displays, Trixie knew the time was ripe to make their move. The world would soon tremble at the might of the Raven Coven, with Samantha as its crown jewel.

But their plans were about to be disrupted by an unexpected confrontation.

Carol, the coven witch who had previously clashed with Samantha and the Shadow Sisters, had been watching the recent developments with a seething resentment. She had not forgotten the humiliation of her defeat, and the sight of Samantha's growing power only fuelled her desire for vengeance.

One day, as Samantha and Trixie were engrossed in a private training session, Carol made her move. She burst into the chamber, her eyes wild with hatred.

"You!" Carol snarled, her gaze fixed on Samantha. "I won't let you get away with this. You and your *precious* Trixie are going to pay for what you've done!"

Trixie immediately stepped in front of Samantha, her features hardening. "Carol, you foolish girl. Do you really think you can challenge us and hope to win?"

Carol's lips curled into a sneer. "I don't care about your power or your precious coven. All I want is to see you *destroyed*."

With a flick of her wrist, Carol unleashed a torrent of dark energy, the purple-black tendrils lashing out towards Trixie and Samantha. Trixie reacted quickly, erecting a shimmering barrier that intercepted the attack, the force of the impact reverberating through the chamber.

Samantha watched, her eyes narrowed, as Trixie and Carol exchanged a series of powerful spells, their magic clashing in a dazzling display of light and shadow. But just as Samantha was about to join the fray, Carol managed to land a devastating blow, sending Trixie flying across the room.

Trixie crashed against the wall, her staff clattering to the floor as she crumpled, unconscious. Samantha felt a surge of rage, her grip tightening around her staff as she advanced on Carol.

"You'll pay for that," Samantha growled, her voice laced with a dark, unforgiving edge.

Carol's eyes widened momentarily, a flicker of fear flashing across her features. But then her expression hardened, and she raised her hands, summoning a maelstrom of dark energy.

What followed was a brutal clash of raw, unbridled power. Samantha's spells were fuelled by the potion's influence, her movements swift and merciless. Carol fought back with everything she had, but she was quickly overwhelmed by the sheer force of Samantha's attacks.

As the battle raged on, the chamber began to crumble around them, the very walls shaking under the strain of the magical onslaught. Samantha unleashed a final, devastating blast, slamming Carol against the floor with enough force to crack the stone.

Carol lay there, battered and bloodied, her chest heaving. Samantha towered over her, her staff raised, poised to deliver the final, fatal blow.

But just before she could act, Carol managed to summon the last of her strength, disappearing in a swirl of dark energy, her agonized cries echoing through the chamber as she fled.

Samantha let out a frustrated growl, her staff clattering to the ground as she turned her attention to the unconscious Trixie. She knelt beside the older witch, her brow furrowed with concern – a rare glimpse of the old Samantha shining through the veil of darkness.

The night of the full moon had arrived, and Samantha found herself standing beneath the massive, gnarled tree that marked the heart of the Raven Coven's territory. The silvery moonlight cast an ethereal glow over the ancient, twisting branches, lending an air of mysticism to the already ominous landscape.

Samantha gazed up at the moon, feeling the raw power of the celestial body pulsing through her veins. She could sense the energy swirling all around her, the very fabric of reality thrumming with the anticipation of the ritual to come.

A sudden movement in the shadows caught her attention, and Samantha tensed, her grip tightening on her staff. But then, a familiar figure emerged, and Samantha's expression softened ever so slightly.

"Trixie," she greeted, her voice tinged with relief. "I was beginning to wonder where you were."

Trixie stepped forward, her expression a mix of annoyance and concern. Propping her up was none other than Carol, the coven witch who had previously clashed with Samantha and the Shadow Sisters.

"Samantha, what is the meaning of this?" Trixie demanded, her brow furrowed. "Why did you leave me behind?"

Carol's eyes narrowed, and she glared at Samantha with a mixture of resentment and trepidation. "Yes, Samantha, what are you playing at? And why is *she* here?"

Samantha's gaze swept over the two witches, her expression unreadable. "The obvious, of course. Tonight is the night of the full moon, the time when our power will be at its peak. Did you think I would let anything – or anyone – stand in my way?"

Trixie's eyes widened, and she tried to take a step forward, but Carol's grip on her kept her in place. "Samantha, you can't be—"

But Samantha raised a hand, silencing her. "Quiet, Trixie. I have work to do."

Without another word, Samantha closed her eyes, focusing her energy. Her entire body began to glow with a pulsing, violet light, and the very air around her crackled with arcane power. Trixie and Carol watched, transfixed, as the magic seemed to channel towards Samantha, strengthening her with each passing second.

Samantha's grip tightened on her staff, and with a sudden, fluid motion, she raised it high, the orb at the tip igniting with a blinding radiance. Trixie and Carol shielded their eyes, the intensity of the light searing their vision.

And then, in a single, swift movement, Samantha brought the staff down, shattering the orb. A shockwave of energy rippled outward, and Samantha felt the magic surge through her, merging with her own in a dizzying rush.

As the light faded, Samantha stood before them, her expression calm and resolute. The staff, now devoid of its power, lay at her feet, forgotten.

Trixie stared at her, her face a mask of horror and disbelief. "Samantha, what have you done?"

Samantha's lips curled into a cold, mirthless smile. "I've taken what is rightfully mine. The time for half-measures is over. Now, the true power of the Raven Coven is mine to wield."

Without another word, Samantha raised her hand, conjuring a shimmering portal. With a final, piercing glance at Trixie and Carol, she stepped through, the portal snapping shut behind her, leaving the two witches in stunned silence.

Trixie's grip on Carol's arm tightened, her mind racing. "This... this was not the plan. Samantha has gone too far, and Malory will not be pleased."

Carol's expression was one of a mixture of awe and trepidation. "What did she do? How could she have become so powerful, so quickly?"

Trixie shook her head, her eyes filled with a rare glimpse of uncertainty. "I fear the answer lies in the potion I gave her. But I never imagined the consequences would be so... drastic."

The two witches stood there, the weight of Samantha's actions weighing heavily upon them. They knew that the world they had once known was about to be turned upside down, and they could only hope that they would be able to contain the destructive force that Samantha had now become.

*

The air was thick with tension as Trixie and Carol waited, their hearts pounding with a mixture of fear and uncertainty. The ritual was meant to be a moment of triumph, a chance for the Raven Coven to fully harness Samantha's power and cement their dominance. But now, with Samantha's sudden and unexpected actions, the future seemed more precarious than ever.

It wasn't long before the sound of approaching footsteps drew their attention, and Malory, the High Priestess of the Raven Coven, emerged from the shadows, her expression a storm of fury and trepidation.

"What is the meaning of this?" Malory demanded, her piercing gaze sweeping over Trixie and Carol. "Where is Samantha? And why have you two been left behind?"

Trixie swallowed hard, her usual confidence shaken. "Malory, I... I'm afraid Samantha has taken matters into her own hands.

She's gone, and she's taken all of the power from her staff, binding it to herself."

Malory's eyes widened, and for a brief moment, the High Priestess's composure cracked, revealing a glimpse of genuine horror. "She's done *what*?" she hissed, her voice laced with a palpable sense of dread.

Carol stepped forward, her expression shifting from awe to alarm. "Malory, Trixie told us that she had given Samantha a potion, one that was meant to strip away her last vestiges of humanity. But…" She glanced at Trixie, her brow furrowing. "There's more to it, isn't there?"

Malory's gaze snapped to Trixie, her eyes narrowed. "Yes, Trixie, do tell us the *full* extent of your meddling."

Trixie swallowed hard, her usual bravado giving way to a rare moment of vulnerability. "I… I gave Samantha the potion, yes. But I didn't realize that you had already tampered with the water she was drinking. The combination of the two…" She trailed off, her face paling.

Malory's expression darkened, and she took a step forward, her robes billowing around her. "The combination of the two *what*, Trixie? Speak up, or so help me, I'll—"

"The combination of the two potions has made Samantha more powerful than any of us could have imagined," Trixie interrupted, her voice trembling. "No one has ever had two doses of such potent magic-enhancing elixirs. Malory, we have no idea what the consequences will be."

Malory's face contorted with a mixture of horror and dread, and for a brief, unsettling moment, the High Priestess seemed to waver, the weight of the revelation shaking her to her core.

"Impossible," she breathed, her hands clenching into fists. "No one has ever survived such a thing. The power would be...unimaginable."

Trixie nodded, her expression grim. "And Samantha has taken that power for herself. She's gone, Malory, and we have no idea where she's headed or what she plans to do with that kind of unchecked magic."

Malory's eyes narrowed, a flicker of determination igniting within them. "Then we must find her, and stop her, before she can unleash her wrath upon the world. The consequences of her actions could be catastrophic."

Carol stepped forward, her features etched with a mix of trepidation and resolve. "Malory, what do you suggest we do? Samantha has become a force to be reckoned with. Even the Shadow Sisters may not be able to stop her now."

Malory's expression hardened, her lips pressed into a thin, determined line. "We have no choice. We must mobilize the full might of the Raven Coven. And we must do it quickly before Samantha's power becomes truly unstoppable."

With a swirl of her robes, Malory turned and strode away, her steps quickening as she disappeared into the shadows. Trixie and Carol exchanged a wary glance, both of them acutely aware of the gravity of the situation they now faced.

The delicate balance of power had been shattered, and the world was about to bear witness to the rise of a sorceress whose thirst for vengeance had been amplified to unprecedented heights. And the Raven Coven, for all their vaunted strength, could only hope that they would be able to contain the destruction that was about to be unleashed.

Chapter 15

The Shadow Sisters, Ember and Jade, approached the ancient, twisted tree, their faces set with grim determination. They had sensed the disturbance in the air, the surge of raw power that had swept through Nepal, and they knew that they could no longer afford to stay on the sidelines.

As they drew closer, it became clear that the Raven Coven was already gathered at the base of the tree, their robes billowing in the cold wind. Trixie and Carol stood apart from the others, both of them looking worse for wear, their expressions etched with a mixture of anger and trepidation.

Ember stepped forward, her eyes narrowing as she surveyed the scene. "Where is Samantha?" she demanded, her voice laced with a barely contained urgency.

Trixie's lips pressed into a thin, unyielding line. "That's none of your concern, Shadow Sister. This is the Raven Coven's business, not yours."

Jade moved to stand beside Ember, her gaze hardening. "The moment Samantha's actions began to threaten the balance of power in Nepal, it became *our* concern. Now, where is she?"

Carol let out a bitter laugh, her eyes glinting with a dangerous light. "Wouldn't you like to know? The little traitor has run off, leaving us to clean up her mess."

Ember's brow furrowed, and she exchanged a troubled look with Jade. "What do you mean, 'her mess'? What has she done?"

Trixie opened her mouth to respond, but Carol cut her off, her voice dripping with venom. "She's done what we should have done from the start – she's taken the power of the Raven Coven for herself. And now, she's gone, leaving us to deal with the consequences."

Jade's eyes widened, and she took a step forward, her expression a mix of shock and dismay. "You mean she's... she's turned against you?"

Trixie's gaze flicked to the side, her usual composure cracking. "It's worse than that. Samantha has found a way to harness the full power of the Raven Coven, binding it to herself. And the consequences of that... we can't even begin to imagine."

Ember's brow furrowed, and she exchanged a weighted look with Jade. "Then we have no choice. We have to find her, and stop her before she can unleash her wrath upon the Nepal."

Jade nodded, her expression grim. "Agreed. But we'll need help – help from those who know Samantha best."

Trixie let out a derisive snort, her eyes narrowing. "And what makes you think *they* can do anything to stop her now? Samantha is beyond your pitiful attempts at redemption."

Ember's gaze hardened, and she took a step forward, her staff at the ready. "Then we'll have to try. Because if Samantha isn't stopped, the consequences will be dire – for all of us."

Trixie's expression darkened, and she raised her staff, the gem at the tip glowing with a menacing light. "You Shadow Sisters have meddled in our affairs for the last time. This ends here."

The air crackled with tension as the two groups faced off, their magic swirling and building, ready to be unleashed. Ember and

Jade braced themselves, their fingers tightening around the familiar grip of their staves.

But just as the first volley of spells was about to be cast, a familiar voice rang out, cutting through the charged atmosphere.

"Wait! Please, you have to listen to us."

Ember and Jade whirled around to see Maggie and Ethan, their expressions a mix of fear and determination, as they pushed their way through the throng of Raven Coven witches.

Trixie's eyes narrowed, and she levelled her staff at the pair. "You two. What possible reason could you have for interfering?"

Maggie stepped forward, her hands raised in a placating gesture. "Because it was our fault. Our betrayal is what drove Samantha into the Raven Coven's arms in the first place. If anyone has a chance of reaching her, it's us."

Ethan nodded, his jaw set with a grim resolve. "We have to try. We owe Samantha that much, at least."

Trixie's grip on her staff tightened, and for a moment, it seemed as though she would unleash her fury upon the two. But then, a flicker of uncertainty crossed her features, and she slowly lowered her weapon.

"Very well," she murmured, her voice barely audible. "But understand this – if you fail, the consequences will be *catastrophic*."

Ember and Jade exchanged a cautious glance, their unease evident. But they knew that Maggie and Ethan were their best hope of reaching Samantha, of bringing her back from the brink of darkness.

With a nod, Ember turned to the Raven Coven, her expression grim. "Then lead the way. We have a sorceress to save."

The Shadow Sisters, along with Maggie and Ethan, surged forward, their determination burning bright even as the weight of the task ahead threatened to crush them.

*

The group followed the trail of devastation, the air thick with the lingering scent of dark magic. As they emerged from the shadows of Nepal, they found themselves in a familiar setting – the very town where Samantha's life had been torn apart.

Maggie and Ethan exchanged a weighted glance, the guilt etched into their features. This was the place where they had betrayed Samantha's trust, shattering the life she had once known.

Ember and Jade scanned their surroundings, their staves at the ready. The town was eerily quiet, the usual hum of activity replaced by an unsettling silence. And then, they spotted her.

Samantha stood in the centre of the town square, her once-vibrant eyes now burning with a fiery, crimson glow. The air around her crackled with raw power, and Maggie felt a chill run down her spine at the sight.

Cautiously, Maggie and Ethan stepped forward, their hands raised in a gesture of peace. "Samantha," Maggie began, her voice tinged with a condescending concern, "we're here to help you. This has all gotten out of hand, but we can fix it. Just come back with us, and we can make things right."

Samantha's gaze narrowed, and she let out a derisive laugh. "Make things *right*?" she sneered, her voice dripping with contempt. "You two couldn't even be *real* friends, let alone fix the mess you've created."

Ethan took a tentative step forward, his expression a mask of contrition. "Samantha, please, we never meant to hurt you. It was a mistake, a lapse in judgment. But we're here now, and we want to help you."

Samantha's eyes flashed with unbridled fury, and she raised a hand, a glowing orb of crimson energy forming in her palm. "Help me?" she spat. "The only thing you two ever did was *betray* me. And now, you think you can just waltz back in and play the heroes?"

Maggie reached out, her voice tinged with desperation. "Samantha, please, we're sorry. We know we hurt you, but we still care about you. We want to make things right, to go back to how things used to be."

Samantha let out a scream of rage, the energy in her hand pulsing with a menacing intensity. "How things used to be?" she snarled. "Those *good times* you're so nostalgic for were all a lie! You were never my true friends, not really. And now, I'll never have to worry about being betrayed again."

With a swift motion, Samantha hurled the energy blast towards Maggie, the crimson orb crackling with power. But before it could reach its target, Ethan dove in front of her, shielding her with his own body.

The blast struck Ethan squarely in the chest, sending him hurtling backwards. He crumpled to the ground, his body convulsing with agonizing spasms as the dark magic coursed through him.

Maggie let out an anguished cry, rushing to his side. "Ethan, no!" she wailed, her hands trembling as she tried to assess the extent of his injuries.

Samantha watched, her expression cold and unforgiving. "That's what you get for trying to play the hero," she hissed. "Now, stay out of my way, *traitor*."

Ember and Jade moved to intercept, their staves raised and ready to defend their friends. But Samantha's power had grown exponentially, and they knew that they would be hard-pressed to match her onslaught.

As the Shadow Sisters braced themselves for the coming onslaught, Maggie cradled the wounded Ethan in her arms, her tears flowing freely. "I'm so sorry, Samantha," she whispered, her voice barely audible. "Please, don't do this. We can still fix this, together."

But Samantha's eyes had turned a deep, crimson red, the last vestiges of her humanity consumed by the dark magic that now flowed unimpeded through her veins. She raised her hand, the energy pulsing and swirling, and Maggie knew that this was no longer the Samantha she had once known.

This was a force of pure, unadulterated darkness – and it was about to be unleashed upon the world.

Chapter 16

Samantha's crimson-hued gaze swept over the Shadow Sisters and her former friends, a malevolent sneer curving her lips. With a casual flick of her wrist, she unleashed a torrent of twisting vines, their thorns dripping with a vicious poison.

Ember and Jade reacted swiftly, erecting a shimmering barrier to shield themselves and Maggie, who cradled the wounded Ethan in her arms. But the poisonous tendrils lashed against the magical shield, probing for weaknesses, their relentless assault fuelled by Samantha's unbridled rage.

"You think your pathetic attempts at magic can stop me?" Samantha spat, her voice echoing with a chilling, otherworldly resonance. "I've surpassed you all, left you behind in the dust. And now, I'll show you the true power of the Raven Coven."

Ember's brow furrowed with concentration as she struggled to maintain the barrier, her own magic straining under the onslaught. "Samantha, please, you have to listen to us. This isn't the way. Let us help you!"

Samantha let out a derisive laugh, her fingers curling as she poured more power into the vines. "Help me?" she scoffed. "The only thing you've ever done is *betray* me. And now, you'll all pay the price."

With a sweeping motion, Samantha directed the poisonous tendrils to ensnare the Shadow Sisters, wrapping them in a choking, constricting embrace. Ember and Jade cried out in pain as the thorns bit into their flesh, their magic faltering under the strain.

Maggie watched in horror, tears streaming down her face. "Samantha, stop! This isn't you, please, you have to fight this!"

But Samantha's expression remained cold and unforgiving. "The old Samantha is gone," she declared, her voice laced with a terrifying finality. "And now, it's time for the world to feel the true power of the Raven Coven."

Turning her attention away from the struggling sorceresses, Samantha raised her hands, a shimmering portal opening at her command. Through the swirling vortex, the unsuspecting citizens of the city below could be seen, going about their daily lives, unaware of the impending doom.

Samantha's eyes narrowed, a cruel smile spreading across her face. "Farewell, my *friends*," she sneered, and with a flick of her wrists, a torrent of dark energy cascaded through the portal, raining down upon the helpless town below.

The air was filled with the agonized cries of the people as they were engulfed by the relentless magical assault. Buildings crumbled, the earth trembled, and chaos erupted as panic seized the populace.

Maggie watched in horror, her heart-shattering at the sight. "Samantha, no!" she screamed, her voice drowned out by the deafening din of destruction.

Ember and Jade, their bodies wracked with pain from the poisonous vines, could only watch in dread as the city descended into a nightmare of Samantha's creation. The power she had unleashed was beyond anything they had ever faced, and they knew, with a sinking feeling, that they were utterly powerless to stop her.

As the chaos below continued to unfold, Samantha stood tall, her expression one of cold, unwavering triumph. The last vestiges of the old Samantha had been consumed by the darkness, leaving behind a force of pure, unrelenting vengeance.

And now, with the full might of the Raven Coven at her command, she was about to show the world the true price of betrayal.

Malory watched in growing horror as Samantha unleashed her dark magic upon the unsuspecting city below, the destruction unfolding with a relentless, unstoppable force. The very ground trembled beneath her feet, and the air crackled with the intensity of the power that had been set loose.

She turned to Trixie, her normally stoic expression etched with a rare glimpse of genuine panic. "This has gone too far. Samantha has become an unstoppable force, and we are powerless to stop her."

Trixie's gaze was torn between pride and trepidation. "But Malory, surely there must be a way to reason with her, to pull her back from the brink. She was once one of us, after all."

Malory's lips pressed into a thin, unyielding line. "You know as well as I do that the potion we gave her, the combination of our own dark magic, has stripped away any vestige of her former self. Samantha is lost to us now."

Carol, her own features a mask of grim realization, stepped forward. "Then what do we do? If we can't stop her, the Nepal – and the mortal realm – will be destroyed."

Malory's gaze drifted to the Shadow Sisters, their bodies ensnared by Samantha's poisonous vines, their magic faltering under the strain. "We have no choice," she admitted, her voice barely above a whisper. "We must ask for their help."

Trixie's eyes widened, and she opened her mouth to protest, but Malory raised a hand, silencing her.

"Trixie, you know as well as I do that Samantha's power has surpassed even our own. We cannot contain her, not anymore. If we have any hope of survival, we must work with the Shadow Sisters to stop her, before she destroys everything in her path."

Trixie's expression wavered, and for a moment, the older witch seemed to waver, the weight of her own actions finally catching up with her. "But... what if it's too late? What if there's no part of the old Samantha left to save?"

Malory's gaze hardened. "Then we must do what is necessary, no matter the cost. The Nepal – and the mortal realm – cannot withstand the full force of Samantha's wrath. We must act before it's too late."

With a resigned sigh, Trixie nodded, her fingers tightening around her staff. "Very well. Let us go to the Shadow Sisters and pray that we can find a way to reach the Samantha we once knew."

Malory swept past her, her robes billowing in her wake. "Pray, indeed. For if we fail, there may be no world left to save."

As the Raven Coven witches approached the struggling Shadow Sisters, Ember and Jade looked up, their expressions a mix of defiance and desperation.

"What do you want?" Jade gasped, her voice strained by the constricting vines.

Malory knelt beside them, her gaze uncharacteristically solemn. "We need your help. Samantha has become a force beyond our control, and if we cannot stop her, the consequences will be catastrophic."

Ember's eyes widened, and she glanced towards the city, where the destruction continued to unfold. "Then you admit that you can't stop her on your own?"

Malory nodded, her pride visibly swallowing her words. "Yes. We need your aid, Shadow Sisters, for the sake of all that we hold dear."

Trixie stepped forward, her expression uncharacteristically vulnerable. "Please, you must help us. Somewhere, deep inside Samantha, there is still a glimmer of the person she once was. If anyone can reach her, it's you."

Jade exchanged a weighted look with Ember, their minds racing. They knew the risks, the dangers that came with facing off against Samantha's unchecked power. But they also knew that they could not simply stand by and watch the world crumble.

With a pained nod, Ember turned to Malory. "Very well. We'll help you, for the sake of all that is at stake. But you must follow our lead, and trust that we know what we're doing."

Malory's lips tightened, but she inclined her head in acknowledgement. "Agreed. Time is of the essence – we must move quickly before Samantha's destruction consumes us all."

As the unlikely allies moved to confront the rampaging sorceress, a glimmer of hope flickered in the shadows. Perhaps, just perhaps, they could still reach the Samantha they had once known and pull her back from the brink of absolute darkness.

The fate of the world now rested in their hands.

*

With a shared sense of purpose, the Shadow Sisters and the Raven Coven witches worked in tandem, their combined magic straining against the choking grip of Samantha's poisonous vines. Ember and Jade, their movements limited by the constricting tendrils, directed Malory and Trixie in weaving a counter-spell, their voices mingling in a chorus of incantations.

Slowly but surely, the vines began to loosen, their hold on the sorceresses weakening. Maggie, her face etched with determination, joined the effort, her fingers tracing arcane symbols in the air to bolster the group's collective power.

Malory's brow furrowed with concentration, her gaze flicking towards the city below, where the destruction continued to unfold. "We must hurry," she urged, her voice laced with a rare note of desperation. "Samantha's rampage knows no bounds."

Trixie's expression was a mixture of guilt and resolve. "Then let us free ourselves and confront her. Perhaps there is still a glimmer of the old Samantha we can reach."

As the last of the vines slithered away, the sorceresses surged forward, their staves raised and their magic crackling to life. Malory's eyes narrowed, her voice ringing out with an uncharacteristic command.

"Samantha!" she called, her words cutting through the chaos. "Cease this madness at once, or we will be forced to stop you."

Samantha's crimson gaze snapped towards them, a twisted smile curving her lips. "Stop me?" she scoffed, her voice laced with a chilling, otherworldly resonance. "You're welcome to try,

Malory, but you'll find that I'm far beyond your pathetic attempts at control."

With a fluid motion, Samantha raised her hands, and the very earth seemed to tremble in response. Ember's eyes widened, and she thrust her staff forward, conjuring a tangled web of vines to ensnare the rogue sorcerers.

But Samantha was faster, her movements a blur of power and precision. She swept her arms in a wide arc, the vines withering to ash before they could reach her.

"Fools," she hissed, her voice dripping with contempt. "Your petty tricks can't hope to match the full might of the Raven Coven."

Trixie stepped forward, her expression a rare mixture of pleading and resolve. "Samantha, please, you must listen to us. This path you've chosen, it will only lead to more pain and destruction. There's still time to turn back, to reclaim the person you once were."

Samantha's eyes narrowed, her gaze sweeping over the assembled witches with a cold indifference. "The person I once was, is *gone*," she declared, her voice ringing with a sense of finality. "I am no longer bound by the weaknesses of the past. I am *power* incarnate, and nothing will stand in my way."

With a flick of her wrist, Samantha conjured a shimmering portal, its edges crackling with raw energy. Malory's eyes widened, and she rushed forward, her staff raised in a desperate attempt to stop the sorceress.

"Samantha, don't do this!" she cried, her voice laced with a rare glimpse of fear. "The destruction you unleash will be beyond our control, beyond *anyone's* control."

But Samantha merely laughed, a chilling, hollow sound that sent shivers down the spines of the gathered witches. "Beyond your control?" she echoed, her voice dripping with disdain. "No, Malory, this is *exactly* what I want."

With a sweeping motion, Samantha rose into the air, her body glowing with an eerie, crimson light. The portal before her widened, and the sorceress raised her hands, a ball of intense, white-hot energy forming between her palms.

"Witness the true power of the Raven Coven," Samantha thundered, her voice echoing across the city. "And know that none shall escape my wrath!"

The energy ball pulsed and swelled, and the Shadow Sisters and Raven Coven witches braced themselves, their staves raised in a desperate attempt to counter the impending onslaught.

As Samantha prepared to unleash her devastating attack, a small glimmer of hope flickered in the hearts of the gathered sorceresses. Perhaps, just perhaps, they could still find a way to reach the Samantha they once knew and pull her back from the brink of total annihilation.

The fate of the world now hung in the balance, and the battle for Samantha's soul was about to reach its climactic conclusion.

Chapter 17

The air crackled with the intensity of Samantha's gathered power, the white-hot energy swirling and pulsing between her outstretched hands. Malory, Trixie, and the Shadow Sisters braced themselves, their staves raised in a desperate attempt to counter the impending onslaught.

"Samantha, please, don't do this!" Ember cried, her voice laced with a mixture of pleading and dread. "You'll destroy everything in your path, including the innocent people below!"

Samantha's crimson gaze narrowed, a twisted smile curving her lips. "That's the idea," she hissed, her voice dripping with malice. "They've had their chance, and they've *failed*. Now, they will all feel the full force of my wrath."

With a deafening crack, Samantha unleashed the energy, a searing torrent of white-hot flames cascading down towards the unsuspecting city below. The sorceresses reacted with lightning speed, their staves weaving intricate patterns as they tried to erect a shielding spell.

But the sheer power of Samantha's attack was overwhelming, shattering their defences like fragile glass. The explosion rocked the very foundations of the earth, sending the covens hurtling backwards, their bodies slamming against the ground with bone-crushing force.

Smoke and debris filled the air, obscuring the devastation that had been unleashed. Coughing and sputtering, the battered sorceresses struggled to their feet, their eyes wide with horror as they surveyed the burning city.

Maggie, her face streaked with grime and tears, turned to Ethan, her expression one of desperate determination. "We have to try, Ethan. We can't just let her destroy everything."

Ethan' jaw tightened, his own features etched with a mixture of fear and resolve. "I know, Maggie. But what can we do? She's beyond our power now."

Jade, her arm hanging limply at her side, staggered towards them, her breathing ragged. "You two... you have to reach her. You're the only ones who might still have a chance."

Trixie, her usual composure shattered, gripped Jade's shoulders, her eyes wild. "But how? Samantha has become a force of pure destruction. She won't listen to reason, not anymore."

Malory, her robes singed, and her features etched with a rare glimpse of despair, stepped forward, her gaze fixed on the raging inferno in the distance. "We have no choice. If we cannot stop her, the entire world will be consumed by her wrath."

Maggie and Ethan exchanged a weighted look, their hearts pounding with a mixture of fear and determination. They knew the risks, the likelihood that Samantha would not – *could* not – be swayed. But they also knew that they owed her this, a final chance to pull her back from the brink.

With a nod, Maggie turned to Malory, her voice surprisingly steady. "Tell us what we need to do."

Malory's eyes narrowed, and she gestured towards the burning city. "Go to her, and appeal to the last vestiges of the person she once was. It's our only hope."

Maggie and Ethan took a deep breath, steeling themselves for the daunting task ahead. As they turned to face the raging inferno, a small, desperate cry suddenly pierced through the chaos, freezing them in their tracks.

Samantha paused, her hands faltering, the swirling energy between her palms flickering and dimming. Her crimson gaze swept across the burning landscape, and for a brief, fleeting moment, a flicker of *something* flickered in her eyes – a glimmer of the Samantha they had once known.

The Shadow Sisters and Raven Coven witches held their breath, their hearts pounding with a renewed sense of hope. Perhaps, just perhaps, there was still a chance to reach her, to pull her back from the brink of total destruction.

Maggie and Ethan exchanged a look, their resolve hardening. This was their moment, their final opportunity to make things right. With a shared nod, they surged forward, their voices mingling in a desperate plea.

"Samantha, *please*! Listen to us!"

The fate of the world now rested on the fragile thread of Samantha's wavering resolve.

Maggie stepped forward, her eyes pleading with Samantha. "Samantha, please, listen to us. You have to stop this – the children, the innocent people, they don't deserve this!"

Samantha's crimson gaze swept over the burning city, the destruction she had unleashed, and for a moment, her expression faltered. Her eyes landed on a small, terrified child trapped amidst the flames, their cries of fear piercing through the chaos.

Maggie seized the opportunity, her voice cracking with emotion. "Samantha, look at them. The babies, the families –

they're suffering because of *us*. Because of what we did to you. But they don't deserve this, Samantha. *No one* does."

Ethan moved to Maggie's side, his own features etched with a rare vulnerability. "Samantha, we know we betrayed you. We know we hurt you in the worst way possible. But this – this isn't the answer. Please, for the sake of everyone, make it stop."

Samantha's hands trembled, the swirling energy between her palms flickering and dimming. The child's cries echoed in her ears, a shattering reminder of the innocence she was about to destroy.

Suddenly, with a surge of determination, Samantha plunged through the roaring flames, her body shielding the child as she pulled them to safety. The Shadow Sisters and Raven Coven witches watched in stunned silence as Samantha emerged from the inferno, the small child cradled in her arms, unharmed.

Samantha's crimson gaze swept over the devastation she had wrought, the realization of her actions crashing down upon her. With an anguished cry, she thrust her hands skyward, summoning a powerful tornado that swept across the city, its swirling winds snuffing out the raging flames.

The sorceresses watched, their expressions a mixture of relief and apprehension, as Samantha rose into the air, the child still clutched protectively against her chest. Without a moment's hesitation, she dove into the depths of the ocean, the crashing waves engulfing her and the flames, extinguishing the last vestiges of the destruction.

Maggie and Ethan stared, their eyes glistening with tears, as the last of the smoke and embers faded into the distance. Malory and Trixie exchanged a weighted glance, their own features etched with a rare glimpse of awe.

"She... she stopped," Jade breathed, her voice barely audible over the sound of the waves.

Ember's brow furrowed, her gaze fixed on the spot where Samantha had disappeared. "But for how long? The darkness within her has grown too powerful to simply be quelled by a single act of conscience."

Malory's lips pressed into a thin, determined line. "Then we must find her and confront her before the darkness consumes her once more. The balance of the Nepal – and the mortal realm – hangs in the balance."

Trixie stepped forward, a glimmer of hope shining in her eyes. "Perhaps there is still a chance to save her. If we can reach the last vestiges of the Samantha we once knew, we may be able to pull her back from the brink."

The Shadow Sisters and Raven Coven witches exchanged a weighted look, the gravity of the situation weighing heavily upon them. They had witnessed the sheer power of Samantha's darkness, the devastation it could wreak. But they had also seen the flicker of her humanity, the glimmer of the person she had once been.

With a renewed sense of purpose, they set off, their staves at the ready, determined to confront Samantha and find a way to bring her back from the edge of oblivion. The fate of the world hung in the balance, and they knew that failure was simply not an option.

As they followed the trail left by Samantha's descent into the ocean, a sense of cautious optimism began to take hold. Perhaps, with their combined efforts, they could still save the Samantha they had once known and prevent the darkness from consuming her – and the world – forever.

*

Samantha stumbled out of the water, her limbs heavy and cold as she took in the destruction around her. The dampness clung to her skin, but the air itself felt hotter, scorched from the flames she had only just extinguished. Small green shoots sprang from the blackened earth as she walked, weaving into a new carpet of life beneath her feet. Each step she took restored something: a wall rebuilt itself, a tree blossomed anew. Her magic worked in quiet, harmonious pulses, breathing life back into everything she'd torn apart.

But the silence that hung over the village was too absolute. It felt empty, haunted.

In the distance, she spotted the child she'd pulled from the flames, cradled in a healer's arms. The girl was silent, her wide eyes fixed on Samantha. They held no gratitude, only fear. Samantha looked away, guilt tightening her throat as the full weight of her actions pressed down on her. She had saved the girl's life—but from the very danger she herself had created. Around her, other villagers stared from a distance, their faces marked with grief, loss, and a quiet, simmering anger.

Samantha's fingers trembled. *This is my doing.*

She forced herself to look back, to take in the charred beams and shattered windows that her magic could not mend. Some damage would never heal, she realized.

As if summoned, the three coven leaders emerged from the gathering crowd. Their gazes were solemn, unreadable, and yet, Samantha could feel the weight of judgment bearing down on her. She felt her own power surge restlessly, as though challenging the silent rebuke, yet she forced herself to remain still.

"Your actions," one of the leaders began, her voice low, "have caused harm that cannot be undone, Samantha."

Samantha clenched her fists, willing herself not to speak, though her heart was pounding. She wanted to tell them that she hadn't meant for this to happen, that she had tried to stop the flames—she had saved the child, hadn't she?

But it wasn't enough. The deaths, the grief—it would never be enough.

Another coven elder stepped forward. "We have deliberated and have no choice. You possess a power too great, and until you learn to control it, it will destroy more than it restores. For your own safety, and for ours, you will be confined."

Samantha's throat went dry. "You're imprisoning me?" Her voice cracked with a mixture of fear and shame.

The leader nodded. "Until you can be sure of yourself. Your actions have proven that your magic is not yet aligned with your will."

Two members of the coven came forward, stepping to either side of her. Samantha's pulse quickened as they escorted her from the ruins of the village. She glanced back, catching the child's gaze one last time, and felt the loss deepen within her—a dark shadow she could not dispel.

As they led her to a room deep within the coven's enclave, Samantha felt the brush of magic seal the walls, a subtle, impenetrable shield. She placed her hand against the smooth surface, her power stirring beneath her fingers, yet it remained locked within her. She couldn't change this.

For the first time, Samantha understood: her magic might be part of her, but the choice of how to wield it was hers—and hers alone.

Chapter 18

As the door to Samantha's cell clicked shut, Trixie's mind churned with a nagging sense of unease. She cast a last glance at Samantha, whose defeated figure sat slumped in the corner, her hands pressed flat against the cell's enchanted walls. Trixie could feel the traces of energy thrumming through the barrier, containing Samantha's volatile power. It was a necessary step—one that had to be taken for the safety of the coven and everyone Samantha had wronged.

But as they turned to leave, a troubling thought took root.

"Trixie," Malony's voice cut into her spiralling thoughts. "Are you listening?"

Trixie blinked, focusing on the elder sorceress. "I… yes, I'm sorry." She hesitated, trying to shake the sense that something was deeply wrong. "Have you seen Carol?"

Malony frowned. "Carol? No. I haven't seen her, not since last night. She may have been preparing the northern warding circles."

But Trixie shook her head. "She wasn't there." She paused, a sudden chill prickling her skin. "It's not just Carol. Elise and Marina—no one's seen them either."

A long, tense silence stretched between them. Trixie could almost see Malony's mind working, calculating possibilities and tracing the lines of what this absence could mean.

Finally, Malony's voice dropped, steely and quiet. "They must still be smarting from their defeat against Samantha." Her gaze hardened. "These three always harboured resentment, but for them to vanish now... Trixie, we may have rebels in our ranks."

A bitter look crossed Trixie's face. "I knew Samantha's power would make her enemies. They'll want to reclaim what they see as their honour—and we could all be in danger because of it."

Malony nodded, her expression tight with resignation. "Then we must stay vigilant. Samantha's confinement is our priority—she cannot afford to escape. Once she's secure, we'll turn our attention to these would-be rebels."

Together, they strode down the dim, winding corridors of the coven's sanctuary, their footsteps echoing through the stone halls. The shadows seemed to shift around them, as if aware of the silent conflict that now lurked within the coven walls.

As they reached the central chamber, Trixie cast a wary glance at the runes sealing Samantha's cell. Her presence behind the barrier thrummed with restrained magic, but the ancient spells held firm, warding against even the strongest powers Samantha might muster.

Malony placed a hand on Trixie's shoulder, her gaze steady. "Prepare yourself. The rebellion may come sooner than we think."

Trixie nodded, her face set with a grim determination. "Then we'll be ready. If Carol and the others seek to test our defences, they'll find they're up against the full might of the coven."

They left Samantha's cell, their minds focused on the battles yet to come—both within and beyond their enchanted walls. The first whispers of civil war stirred in the coven's depths, unseen but undeniable, as they prepared for what would inevitably follow.

*

The dimly lit chamber was thick with silence, save for the hushed whispers of Carol and her two companions. Hidden deep in a forgotten corner of the coven's sanctuary, they gathered in the flickering candlelight, their faces cast in shadow. Fury simmered in Carol's eyes, glinting like embers waiting to spark into flames.

"Can you believe it?" Carol sneered, voice dripping with contempt. "They lock her away, but not a word to us after we did the dirty work for them. Humiliated us. And for what? For failing to defeat Samantha?"

Marina, the eldest of the three, nodded, her eyes cold and calculating. "They think we're cowards because we couldn't best her power. But now she's trapped, and all that power of hers is behind walls, ripe for the taking."

Beside her, Elise smirked, drawing a small, singed piece of parchment from her cloak. The edges were scorched and curled, and the symbols etched upon it seemed to pulse with a dark, alluring energy. She held it up between her fingers, letting the dim candlelight illuminate its cryptic marks.

Carol's gaze sharpened as she reached for the parchment. "Is that...?"

Elise grinned, handing her the slip of paper. "The spell. The very one Samantha used to absorb the coven's magic. She left traces of it scattered in her wake, singed into the stones and air. It took some work to capture it, but here we are."

Carol's eyes widened, a twisted smile spreading across her face. She clutched the paper as if it were a lifeline, the possibilities whirling through her mind. "So, Samantha thought she could use this to gain the upper hand. But now, with her locked away, it's our turn."

Marina's voice was sharp with bitter amusement. "The irony. She'll be helpless behind those walls, while her own spell fuels our strength."

"And Trixie," Elise muttered, her tone venomous. "She didn't even try to help us when Samantha tore through our defences. All that talk about loyalty and sisterhood... Trixie and her precious Shadow Sisters abandoned us to fend for ourselves."

Carol's fingers tightened around the parchment, her knuckles white. "They'll pay for that betrayal. First, we'll drain Samantha's magic, leaving her weaker than the helpless child she once was. And then..." She trailed off, her eyes narrowing. "Then we'll deal with Trixie and her little sisterhood."

Marina leaned forward, her voice low and fervent. "Imagine it: with Samantha's power, the three of us will be unstoppable. We'll command the shadows and control the coven itself. And Trixie will be powerless to stop us."

Elise's smirk widened. "They're so focused on keeping Samantha locked away, they'll never see us coming."

Carol's eyes glittered with anticipation as she tucked the spell into the folds of her cloak. "Then it's settled. We let them think we're cowed, beaten. And when the time is right, we'll show them what true power looks like."

The three exchanged a dark, satisfied look, their pact sealed in the dim silence. With Samantha's own magic at their fingertips, the seeds of rebellion were sown, ready to take root and bring ruin upon their enemies.

*

Maggie paced the narrow corridor, her arms crossed tightly over her chest, the distant echoes of the coven's whispered conversations reverberating around her. Samantha was locked away, confined to a cell under layers of magical wards. The consequences of her actions—and theirs. The realization had begun to sink in, deeper and heavier with every passing hour.

"She's locked up because of us," Maggie murmured, almost to herself. Her gaze was distant, fixed on some point in the shadows. "Because of what we did."

Ethan leaned against the wall, watching her with a mixture of defensiveness and guilt. "She went too far, Maggie. She nearly killed us both. I don't think we should be blaming ourselves for her choices."

Maggie stopped pacing, her sharp gaze pinning him in place. "And we didn't go too far? You broke her trust, Ethan. You crossed lines, pushed boundaries, and never once thought about what it would do to her. Or to me, for that matter."

Ethan swallowed, his eyes dropping to the floor. He'd heard this all before, but it stung differently now. Watching Samantha's face as the coven had led her away had stirred something unfamiliar in him—a sense of responsibility, of real, unshakable guilt.

"I'm not saying I wasn't wrong," he said, his voice unsteady. "But Maggie... she's dangerous now. Even if we didn't mean to hurt her, this—this isn't all on us."

"Maybe not all," Maggie conceded, her tone softening. "But don't you see it, Ethan? You don't think before you act. You didn't think before you broke her trust, and you certainly didn't think about what it would do to us." She took a step toward him, her gaze unwavering. "It's like you've never cared how your actions affect other people."

He flinched at that. A thousand retorts sprang to mind, but he bit them back, searching for words that wouldn't come off as defensive or dismissive. "I know I messed up. But I stood by you, didn't I? When she attacked, I... I put my life on the line to protect you."

Maggie's expression softened, a flicker of appreciation in her eyes. "You did, Ethan. And I saw that." She took his hand, her grip firm but tinged with sadness. "But protecting me once doesn't erase everything you've done. If we're going to stay together, things have to change."

He looked up at her, his brows furrowing. "What do you mean?"

Maggie exhaled slowly, her tone steely yet calm. "I mean boundaries, Ethan. I mean respecting me, respecting the people in our lives, and learning from your mistakes. If you can't do that, then... we're done."

The finality of her words hung in the air, a line drawn sharply in the sand. Ethan felt the weight of it, understanding for the first time how close he was to losing her—losing everything. He swallowed, nodding.

"I get it, Maggie. I know I've been selfish... careless. But this, with Samantha and everything else—it's a wake-up call. I don't want to be that guy anymore." His voice wavered, the words tinged with a rare vulnerability. "I want to be better, for you. For us."

Maggie's face softened, and she offered him a small, tentative smile. "Then show me, Ethan. Actions speak louder than words."

She tightened her hold on his hand, her gaze unwavering. "This is your last chance. Don't waste it."

Ethan nodded, a glint of determination flickering in his eyes. "I won't."

The two stood there, silent but united, ready to face the consequences of their actions together. It wasn't forgiveness, not yet—but it was a start.

Chapter 19

The Shadow Sisters and Raven Coven gathered in the great hall, its high, arched ceiling echoing their whispered deliberations. Malony stood at the centre of the table, her expression taut as she looked from face to face, each coven member tense with the gravity of their discussion. Trixie watched her with narrowed eyes, arms crossed as she listened closely, considering the implications of every word.

Carol's betrayal hung in the air like an unspoken accusation.

"They've gone silent," Malony began, her voice carrying through the room. "Carol, Elise, Marina—all vanished without a trace. The wards detected no activity. Either they're truly gone, or they're biding their time."

Jade, one of the Shadow Sisters, leaned forward, her gaze icy. "They'll resurface eventually, especially if they believe they're being hunted. And if we move too quickly, we may just drive them deeper underground."

Ember shook her head. "Let them go, let them fume—this is about pride more than vengeance. They're angry that Samantha outmatched them, that they were cast aside after years of loyalty. But that anger may fade. Maybe they just need time to lick their wounds."

Trixie, who had been silent until now, spoke up, her tone sharp. "And if it doesn't fade? Carol has shown she's willing to go against the coven. Now she has access to dangerous spells, and she's had months to nurse her grudge. If we leave them unchecked, we risk far worse than a mutiny."

A murmur ran through the room, half in agreement, half in concern. Malony considered this, her gaze fixed on the distant wall as she weighed the risks.

"They were once loyal," Malony said at last, her tone wary. "If we act too swiftly, we confirm their fears that we see them as threats. It could drive them to rebellion before they're ready."

"But if we do nothing," Trixie interjected, "and they come back with enough strength to rival us? We would be fighting a battle on two fronts—Samantha in her cell, and Carol with her allies."

Ember crossed her arms, her expression one of resigned frustration. "So, we wait. Give them time to return and let them come to us if they choose. But if they don't…"

Malony raised a hand, her face set in a reluctant frown. "Then we take precautions. I propose an alternative."

The room fell silent, all eyes on her.

"We bind their powers if they return and refuse to cooperate. Failing that, we remove them from the coven. Permanently." Malony's voice was steady but edged with a hardness that was impossible to miss.

Trixie's brow furrowed. "Are you suggesting we strip them of their magic entirely?"

"If it comes to that, yes," Malony replied, meeting her gaze without flinching. "But there's another possibility we should consider, one that could strengthen us all. A merger. Both covens united under one leadership. Our collective power would make us a force, too strong for anyone, even Carol, to challenge."

A heavy silence followed her words, each sister weighing the proposal.

Ember's gaze flickered between Malony and Trixie. "You think we can trust each other enough for that? Our ways are different, and uniting the covens may bring its own share of trouble."

"It's a risk," Malony admitted. "But if we're to withstand whatever may come—Carol, Samantha, or something else entirely—we need unity. It would mean protection. Survival."

Jade, her face thoughtful, nodded slowly. "There's truth in that. Alone, either of our covens could fall to the likes of Carol and her followers. Together, we have a chance to outlast and overcome."

Trixie considered this, her expression softening just a fraction. "An alliance," she murmured. "Yes, I see the benefit. But we must be clear on leadership and boundaries if this is to work. Each coven must retain its traditions—there can't be friction over every decision."

Malony inclined her head, acknowledging the concern. "Agreed. We keep our traditions but share our resources, our knowledge, and our defences. As one coven, we are stronger."

After a long pause, Ember nodded, her expression resigned but resolute. "Then let it be so. Let the Shadow Sisters and the Raven Coven join as one. If Carol returns, she'll find we're ready for her."

One by one, the heads of each coven rose in agreement, and Trixie, casting a final wary glance at Malony, extended her hand. Malony met her gesture, clasping her forearm in a firm grip.

"Together, we will prevail," Malony said, her voice steady and certain. And with that, the pact was made, a new alliance forged in the flickering shadows of the coven's halls.

*

The silence in Samantha's cell was thick, pressing in from all sides. Magic pulsed softly around her, woven through the walls and ceiling, a reminder of her captivity. She'd been pacing the small space, trying to keep her mind sharp, though fatigue weighed heavily on her. Each time her hand brushed the enchanted barrier, the energy crackled against her skin, an unyielding wall between her and the world outside.

Suddenly, the quite broke. The heavy door creaked open, and the dim glow of the outer hallway spilled into her cell. Samantha froze, turning toward the doorway.

A familiar figure stood there, silhouetted by the light. Her mother.

Samantha's breath caught in her throat. She hadn't seen her mother since the first inkling of magic had drawn her into this tangled, dangerous path. Maggie and Ethan had told her, in vague words, about her mother's reaction, but Samantha hadn't believed them. She'd convinced herself it was just one more lie in the web they'd spun around her.

But now, seeing her mother standing there, wide-eyed and pale, the truth was undeniable.

"Samantha..." Her mother's voice was barely a whisper, tinged with a horror she made no attempt to hide. She stepped closer, her gaze fixed on the shield that held Samantha captive, as if the barrier itself had inflicted some new wound.

"Mom..." Samantha's voice trembled, a mixture of shame and confusion rising in her chest. "I didn't know you'd... come."

Her mother shook her head, her hands clasping tightly together, knuckles white. "They told me what happened,

Samantha. But I... I couldn't believe it. I didn't want to believe it."

Samantha looked away, her jaw clenching as guilt gnawed at her. "You think I wanted this? That I wanted to hurt people?" She met her mother's gaze, her eyes flashing with a defensive spark. "It wasn't supposed to be this way. I didn't mean for any of it to happen."

Her mother's face softened, but the horror remained in her eyes. "But it did happen, Samantha. Lives were lost. And here you are... locked away like a criminal." She choked on the last word, as though the very thought was too painful to bear.

Samantha's anger wavered, replaced by a hollow ache that she couldn't ignore. "I saved people, too. I stopped the flames. I... I didn't just destroy."

"But at what cost?" Her mother's voice cracked, the words edged with grief. She stepped closer, her hand hovering over the barrier as though she wanted to reach out to her daughter, to touch her, to erase the wall between them. "Samantha, this... this power of yours—it's consuming you. And it's hurting everyone around you."

Samantha's chest tightened, a flicker of defiance rising up, but she bit it back. She didn't want to lash out, not at her mother. She wanted to explain, to tell her the story from the beginning, to make her understand. But where would she even start?

"I thought I was doing something good. I thought... maybe I could control it," she said finally, her voice barely above a whisper.

Her mother's eyes filled with tears, her hand pressing softly against the barrier. "You're my daughter. I've always believed in you. But the person I see here... I don't even recognize her." Her voice dropped to a pained whisper. "What happened to the girl who wanted to help others, who cared about the world around her?"

Samantha felt a sharp pang in her chest, and she looked away, blinking back tears of her own. "She's still here, Mom. She's just... lost."

A long silence stretched between them, the barrier between them more than just a wall of magic. Finally, her mother spoke, her voice steady, if heavy with sorrow.

"Then find her, Samantha. I don't know what's going to happen to you now, but please—if there's any part of that girl left in you, don't let her disappear."

Samantha pressed a hand to the barrier, mirroring her mother's touch on the other side. "I'll try," she whispered, her voice breaking. "I'll try."

Her mother nodded, her expression torn between hope and despair. She lingered for a moment, then stepped back, her gaze fixed on Samantha as though memorizing her face.

Without another word, she turned and walked away, her figure fading into the darkness of the corridor, leaving Samantha alone once more, the ache of her mother's words sinking deeper into her heart.

*

Time drifted in endless silence, punctuated only by the faint hum of magic coursing through the walls of Samantha's cell. Shadows pooled in the corners, the dim light from the single overhead lantern casting a cold, muted glow. Alone, she couldn't escape the sharp ache of her mother's words.

As the hours slipped by, Samantha's stomach clenched, a reminder that it had been too long since she'd eaten anything. She glanced at the small panel beside the door—a button installed to signal for the most basic of requests.

With a sigh, she pressed it.

Minutes passed, each one dragging on longer than the last, until at last, the cell door clicked. Trixie's silhouette appeared on the other side, the latch on a small compartment sliding open with a metallic scrape. Samantha caught a faint scent of something warm—vegetables and herbs, a reminder of the world outside.

Without a word, Trixie slid the tray through the hatch. Samantha stepped forward, lifting the tray and meeting Trixie's gaze through the barrier.

"Thank you," Samantha murmured, her voice quiet but laced with something closer to her old self. She set the tray down, but Trixie didn't leave. Instead, she lingered by the hatch, watching Samantha with a wary, assessing expression.

"There's been news," Trixie began, her voice even but edged with something Samantha couldn't quite place. "Carol and a few members of the Raven Coven have disappeared. They left without a trace—no word, no explanation. Malony and I fear they're planning something."

Samantha straightened, setting down her fork. "Carol went rogue?"

"Yes. And after everything that's happened, it's not a comforting thought." Trixie paused, folding her arms. "The covens have merged, the Shadow Sisters and the Raven Coven. We'll be working as one, moving forward."

Samantha nodded slowly, taking in the news. The idea of a merged coven was significant—it represented a strength she hadn't expected them to muster. But Carol and her allies were another matter. That was power on the loose, dangerous, untamed.

And, maybe, it was an opportunity.

Trixie seemed to study her, waiting for some reaction. "Well?" she asked finally. "Does any of this even matter to you now?"

Samantha glanced down at her tray, a spark of hope igniting within her—a faint possibility, just a whisper of a thought. If Carol was out there, unchecked and angry, she could become a threat to the coven itself. A threat that Samantha, even in her confinement, might be able to counter.

"Yes," she said, her voice soft. "It matters."

Trixie watched her with narrowed eyes, then finally nodded. "Good. You're not as detached as I thought." She stepped back, her silhouette slipping out of sight as she shut the hatch, leaving Samantha in silence once more.

As Samantha picked at the food, her mind turned over the possibilities, her thoughts coalescing around a single idea. If Carol did bring trouble to the coven—if her rebellion threatened to unravel everything—then Samantha might have a chance. A chance to prove that she wasn't just a destroyer. That she could help, could make a difference.

That maybe, somehow, she could still be redeemed.

Chapter 20

The air in the training grounds felt lighter, the weight of constant vigilance lifting ever so slightly. Over a month had passed since the merging of the Shadow Sisters and the Raven Coven, and the alliance was beginning to feel almost natural. In the early days, tension had simmered beneath the surface, as members eyed one another with scepticism and the memory of Carol's defection haunted them. But as the days turned into weeks with no sign of Carol or her rogue allies, the merged coven began to settle into a wary comfort.

Malony, observing the new recruits from the sidelines, allowed herself a small, private sigh of relief. Carol's threat seemed to have vanished, and while they all knew better than to completely drop their guard, a quiet, cautious optimism had taken root. Rumours had even begun to circulate that Carol, and the others had abandoned magic altogether, leaving behind the path of sorcery in favour of obscurity and safety.

"I mean, can you blame them?" Ember muttered to Trixie as they watched a group of young coven members practice defensive spells across the training field. "After all that happened, I wouldn't blame them if they've run off somewhere to hide and pretend to be normal."

Trixie gave a faint nod, her gaze following the precise movements of a pair of students casting warding circles against dark magic. "It's possible. They were humiliated, outcast. I'd probably want to disappear too if it meant saving face."

Jade, who was leading the current session, guided two of the students through a series of shielding techniques, her voice calm but firm. "Remember, the key to protecting yourself against dark magic lies in stability, not power. You must anchor yourself, focus, and keep your energy grounded."

Around her, the students followed her instruction, their expressions intent as they concentrated on conjuring their shields. The shimmering barriers flickered to life, steady and controlled, shimmering with faint hues of green and blue. The coven had grown stronger over the past month, their training against dark magic becoming a daily ritual, a routine. It had started as a precaution, a defence in case Samantha ever broke free from her magical confinement.

But now, with the constant tension easing, the training was beginning to feel more like a set of skills, a practice—rather than a true, imminent preparation for battle.

Ember crossed her arms, her gaze sweeping over the field. "It's ironic, isn't it? We were so focused on Carol's potential return, on keeping watch for her or Samantha to go rogue… but the real threat might already be over."

Trixie nodded slowly, a hint of something unreadable in her expression. "Perhaps. Or maybe they're just lying low, waiting for the right moment."

But the words felt hollow, an echo of her earlier fears that she no longer truly believed. If Carol and her allies had wanted to strike, surely, they would have done so by now. Why wait? Why allow the covens to grow stronger, to unite and train against the very magic they might wield?

Another round of training exercises began, and the students dispersed to practice one-on-one. There were even a few laughs shared between the younger members, a rare sound in recent months. Malony watched them, her heartwarming at the sight.

For the first time in a long time, there was an ease to their interactions, a camaraderie that spoke of resilience and renewal.

"They're getting better," Trixie observed, a faint smile crossing her lips. "Stronger, more confident."

"Yes," Malony agreed, a touch of pride in her voice. "Maybe we can afford to let down our guard a little."

And for the first time in weeks, as the members of the merged coven trained together, learned together, and slowly found a new rhythm, the fear of Carol's return seemed like a distant, faded memory.

*

The sky was painted in deep hues of purple and grey as Carol and her two companions, Mia and Alaric, made their way through the forest toward the ancient tree. They walked in silence at first, the air heavy with unspoken tension. Shadows fell long across their path, and the tree loomed ahead, its gnarled branches twisting toward the sky like skeletal fingers, stark against the fading light. The three had stood under this very tree a month before, nursing wounds of defeat. But tonight, they returned not as victims but as hunters, each with vengeance burning in their veins.

Mia broke the silence first, her voice sharp with bitter resolve. "They thought they could just cast us out," she muttered, her eyes narrowing as she looked up at the tree, "humiliate us in front of everyone…"

Alaric snorted, his lips curling into a sneer. "And now they're all smug, thinking we've slunk away to lick our wounds. Tonight, we'll show them who they should be afraid of."

Mia clenched her fists, her mouth twisted in a dark smile. "Imagine their faces when they realize their power won't save them this time," she said, her voice barely above a whisper. The thrill of revenge crackled between them, feeding their courage.

Carol walked a few paces behind them, her expression oddly serene. She seemed detached, her gaze distant as if lost in thought, though her lips curled with the faintest hint of a smile. It was her idea to meet tonight, to carry out the plan they had only spoken of in whispers. Yet now, as her friends raged beside her, she looked almost... amused.

They reached the tree and stopped. Mia and Alaric turned to Carol, looking to her for direction. She stepped forward, brushing her fingers lightly over the rough bark. A shiver ran through her, and her eyes sparkled with a strange intensity. It was as though the tree were more than a symbol of their past defeat; it was a promise of something new, something powerful.

"Tonight, we won't be leaving empty-handed," Carol murmured, her voice soft but filled with an edge that neither Mia nor Alaric noticed.

Alaric grinned, feeding off her confidence. "They'll regret underestimating us, especially after what we're about to do."

Mia nodded, her eyes flashing with excitement. "Carol, how exactly are we going to do this? Samantha had her staff to channel the magic last time, but we don't have—"

Carol held up a hand, silencing her. "We don't need any trinkets tonight," she said smoothly. Her eyes darkened as she glanced between her two friends. "We're going to make a much stronger connection than that."

Mia and Alaric exchanged a look, momentarily puzzled, but neither dared question her. Carol's words lingered in the air like a spark ready to ignite, and though the thought flitted through their minds that she was holding something back, their hunger for power pushed it aside.

As the first stars began to emerge in the sky above, Carol's smile grew, her gaze locked on the tree as if she could already see the magic that would soon be hers.

*

Shadows pooled around them, deepening as the light faded and the first stars flickered in the evening sky. The tree felt alive somehow, as if it remembered—a silent witness to their bitter defeat. Now it seemed to watch them with a knowing air, waiting for the spell they had planned to summon.

Mia rubbed her arms, shivering slightly. She glanced at Carol, who was still touching the tree's bark, her fingers trailing over it as though it were something precious. Carol's face was illuminated by the last rays of dusk, her expression unreadable, a slight smile tugging at the corners of her mouth. It was a look that made Mia pause, a flicker of doubt creeping into her thoughts.

"Carol, how long will the ritual take?" Mia's voice was hesitant, almost breaking the hush around them.

Carol turned, her gaze sharp as she looked back at her friends. "It won't take long," she replied, her tone calm, almost soothing. "The power is already here, waiting to be claimed. All we have to do is take it."

Alaric grinned, oblivious to Mia's unease. He held his hands out in front of him, flexing his fingers as though he could feel the magic crackling just beyond his reach. "And they won't see it coming," he murmured. "I can almost imagine it—their faces when we return, stronger than ever."

A hint of pride flickered in Carol's eyes, but there was something else beneath it—a glint of satisfaction that seemed too intense, too personal. She spoke slowly, letting each word sink into the cold air around them. "After tonight, we'll be unstoppable."

The words sent a chill through Mia, though she couldn't quite say why. She glanced at Alaric, who was staring at the tree with a look of fierce concentration, clearly imagining the magic they'd soon wield. Mia tried to shake off the feeling, telling herself it was just nerves. But when her gaze returned to Carol, she saw something that made her breath catch—a look so intense it bordered on hunger, a darkness in her eyes that was both unfamiliar and unsettling.

"Are... are you sure we don't need anything to channel the power, Carol?" Mia asked, her voice barely a whisper. "I mean, Samantha had her staff to help her last time. We don't have anything like that."

Carol's smile widened ever so slightly, though there was no warmth in it. "Tonight, we don't need staffs or wands. We're going to use something much... stronger."

Mia felt her heart pound, and a prickle of unease crept up her spine. She glanced at Alaric, but he hadn't noticed the change in Carol's tone. He seemed entranced by the thought of the power they'd gain. The shadows around them seemed to thicken, the wind falling still as though the entire forest were holding its breath, waiting for something dark and inevitable.

Alaric finally broke the silence, stepping forward and placing his hand on the tree beside Carol's. "So, how does this work?" he asked, eagerness in his voice. "Do we just... reach out for the power?"

Carol looked at him, her eyes narrowing. "Something like that," she replied, her voice smooth, velvety. She placed her hand over his, a strange look of satisfaction in her gaze. "Trust me. When the time is right, you'll feel it."

Her hand lingered on his for a moment longer than necessary, and Alaric pulled his fingers back, casting her a questioning look. But Carol didn't seem to notice. She turned back to the tree, her eyes gleaming, her breathing quickening as if she could already feel the magic stirring beneath her skin.

The last traces of light faded, and the forest seemed to close in around them. Mia's heart raced as she watched Carol, feeling a growing sense of unease. There was something about the way Carol moved, the way she looked at them both, that made her feel as though they were missing something, some crucial detail. A small voice in the back of her mind urged her to run, to question Carol, but the promise of power kept her silent.

Carol raised her arms, her voice low and firm as she began to chant, her words mingling with the night air like dark smoke. The tree seemed to respond, its branches rustling softly despite the stillness around them, its roots almost pulsing beneath the ground. Mia shivered, a deep, instinctual fear prickling at her senses. She looked at Alaric, but he was completely absorbed, his eyes fixed on Carol, drawn in by the spell she was weaving.

As Carol continued, the feeling of dread within Mia intensified. Her heart pounded as she glanced around, her mind racing. *What's wrong with me?* she thought, trying to shake off the feeling. But when she looked at Carol's face, illuminated only by starlight, she saw something dark and triumphant in her gaze—a look of pure, unguarded hunger.

Mia took a step back, the weight of realization starting to dawn on her.

Chapter 21

The moon had risen, casting a pale glow over the clearing. Its light seeped through the branches of the ancient tree, illuminating the three figures standing beneath it. Mia shifted uncomfortably, her gaze darting between Carol and Alaric. Something was wrong; she could feel it—an unease prickling at her skin. Carol stood at the centre of the clearing, her back to them, her arms raised toward the moon. But unlike last time, she held nothing in her hands—no staff, no talisman, no object to channel the magic.

Mia cleared her throat, her voice barely breaking the silence. "Carol… what are you absorbing magic from?"

Carol didn't respond. She continued her chant, her voice rising and falling in a language Mia didn't recognize. The strange words seemed to echo, vibrating through the air and making the hair on the back of her neck stand up.

Alaric glanced at Mia, a look of confusion on his face. He opened his mouth as if to speak, but then his eyes widened. Thin streams of light had begun to swirl around them, winding through the air like threads of silver mist. Mia's heart raced as she watched the strands wrap around her arms, her legs, her chest, binding her in place.

"Carol!" Alaric shouted, his voice thick with alarm. "What's happening?"

Carol ignored him, her chant growing louder, more intense. The swirling light tightened around Mia, pressing against her limbs until she could barely move. Panic surged through her as she struggled against the invisible bonds, but it was as if the very air had solidified, trapping her in place. The light began to pulse, each beat draining her strength, leaving her feeling hollow, like something essential was slipping away.

"Carol!" Mia cried, her voice trembling with fear. "What are you doing? Why can't I move?"

Still, Carol continued, her voice steady, unyielding. The words she spoke seemed to seep into Mia's mind, drowning out her thoughts, filling her with a chilling emptiness. She fought against the sensation, her breaths coming in short gasps.

"Carol, please!" Alaric's voice had risen to a desperate pitch. He strained against the light binding him, his face twisted with fear. "Stop this! Tell us what's going on!"

But Carol didn't stop. Her eyes were half-closed, a look of deep concentration on her face as she directed the magic. The light tightened again, forcing a strangled cry from Mia's throat. She felt the energy draining from her, seeping into the strands of magic that bound her, slipping from her body like sand through her fingers.

"Carol!" she screamed, her voice hoarse, tears stinging her eyes. "We're supposed to be friends! Why are you doing this?"

For a moment, Carol's chanting paused. She turned slowly to face them, her eyes glinting in the moonlight, her expression cold and unfeeling. Her gaze flickered over Mia and Alaric, almost dismissive, as though they were merely obstacles to be dealt with. Her lips curled into a small, triumphant smile.

And then, Mia understood.

The realization hit her with the force of a blow, knocking the air from her lungs. She felt her legs weaken beneath her, though the magic held her upright. Carol wasn't drawing from some unseen source of power; she was drawing from *them*.

*

Mia's body tensed as she struggled against the magic, her muscles straining, but it was like fighting against iron chains. The invisible bonds held her in place, tightening with each passing moment. She could feel the last traces of her magic slipping away, draining into the silver threads that connected her to Carol. Panic clawed at her, but she was powerless to move, trapped as surely as if she'd been bound in stone.

Alaric fought beside her, his face pale, his eyes wide with desperation. He tried to lift his hands, his lips moving as he whispered a counterspell, but his voice faltered, growing weaker with every word. His arms dropped back to his sides, limp, as though all strength had been drained from him.

"Carol…" he rasped, his voice barely more than a whisper. But Carol's expression remained cold, detached, as though they were strangers to her. She continued her incantation, her words growing softer now, like a lullaby guiding them to an inevitable end.

Mia's vision blurred, and her knees buckled. The last of her magic flickered within her, faint as a dying ember. She felt the light tighten around her, pulling the final threads of power from her core. Her body grew heavier, weaker, her thoughts slipping away like water through cupped hands.

With one last, strained effort, she turned her gaze to Carol. "Please…" she whispered, her voice breaking. But Carol didn't respond. Her eyes were closed, her hands raised as the magic swirled around her, filling her with the power she had taken.

And then, with a final pulse, the magic was gone.

Mia and Alaric fell to the ground with a heavy, lifeless thud. The impact jolted through Mia's body, but she was too weak to feel the pain. Her vision darkened, the world fading into a blur of shadows and distant stars. Somewhere nearby, she heard the faint sound of Alaric's laboured breathing before it too faded away, slipping into silence.

Carol stood over them, looking down with a faint smile. She took a step forward, her eyes gleaming with an unnatural light as she gazed at her fallen friends. For a moment, she simply watched them, her expression unreadable. Then she crouched beside them, her voice soft, almost affectionate.

"It's because we're friends that you're allowed to live," she murmured, brushing a stray strand of hair from Mia's face. "Consider it a parting gift."

She rose gracefully, barely sparing them another glance as she took a step back. She closed her eyes, letting the rush of power pulse through her veins, feeling it expand and settle within her. The magic was stronger, richer than anything she had ever known, thrumming beneath her skin like a heartbeat. It surged and twisted within her, each sensation vivid, electric. She could feel the energy crackling at her fingertips, whispering promises of things she had only ever dreamed of.

A slow, satisfied smile spread across her face. She lifted one hand, letting a flicker of light dance between her fingers. The sensation was intoxicating, the power hers to command, to wield as she pleased. She glanced at her surroundings, taking in the tree, the silver moonlight casting shadows over the clearing. Everything seemed sharper, clearer, as though the world had shifted to match the intensity of the magic within her.

Carol's triumphant laughter echoed through the shadows as she stepped away from the motionless forms of Mia and Alaric, her body thrumming with the power she had stolen. But the insatiable hunger within her was not yet sated.

With a predatory gleam in her eyes, Carol turned her gaze to the surrounding forest, her senses probing the darkness for any sign of additional prey. It was then that she detected the faint pulse of magic, a siren's call that beckoned her ever closer.

Swiftly, she followed the trail, her movements swift and sure as she navigated the twisting paths. Finally, she emerged into a small clearing, where two young witches huddled around a small campfire, their hushed voices carrying on the cold night air.

"Did you feel that?" one of the girls whispered, her eyes wide with apprehension. "It felt like... like something was watching us."

The other nodded, her fingers tightening around the amulet that hung at her throat. "We should get out of here. This place doesn't feel right."

But before they could react, Carol stepped forward, her presence commanding their attention.

"Well, well," she purred, her voice dripping with false sweetness. "What do we have here? Two little witches, all alone in the dark."

The girls sprang to their feet, their expressions etched with fear as they beheld Carol's imposing figure.

"Who are you?" one of them demanded, her voice trembling. "What do you want?"

Carol's lips curled into a cruel smile. "What do I want?" she echoed, her gaze sweeping over them with a predatory hunger. "Why, I want your power, my dear."

With a flick of her wrist, she unleashed a torrent of dark energy, the crackling tendrils enveloping the young witches before they could react. Their anguished cries pierced the night as Carol drained them of their magic, the power flowing into her like a rising tide.

When the last vestiges of their strength had been siphoned away, the girls crumpled to the ground, their bodies drained and lifeless. Carol stood over them, her eyes gleaming.

"Ah, that's better," she murmured, flexing her fingers as the new power coursed through her. "But I'm still not satisfied."

With a calculated gaze, she turned her attention back toward the city, her mind already focused on her next targets. The Shadow Sisters and their coven would soon feel the full force of her wrath, and there would be no mercy this time.

*

A faint chill clung to the early morning air as Mia stirred, her cheek pressed against the cold, damp earth. She opened her eyes slowly, blinking against the dim grey light seeping through the trees. The sky was paling on the horizon, signalling the approach of dawn, though the clearing remained wrapped in the deep shadows cast by the ancient tree.

Beside her, Alaric lay sprawled on the ground, his face pale and ashen. He stirred as she shifted, his eyes fluttering open, unfocused and hollow. They stared at each other in silence for a moment, the weight of what had happened settling over them like a heavy fog.

Mia sat up slowly, her limbs weak and stiff. She placed a hand on her chest, her fingers pressing against her heart, as if trying to grasp something that was no longer there. There was an emptiness within her, a hollow ache that throbbed beneath her ribs, deeper than any physical pain. Her magic, the essence of who she was, had been ripped from her—drained away, leaving only a cold void in its place.

Alaric's hand trembled as he placed it against the ground, trying to summon the faintest spark of power, but there was nothing. He looked down at his hand, his brow furrowing as he struggled to make sense of it. "Mia... do you... feel anything?" he asked, his voice hoarse and barely a whisper.

Mia shook her head, her eyes wide and fearful. "No... I can't feel anything. It's all gone. She... she took everything." She swallowed, her throat tight as the weight of realization settled over her. "We have nothing left."

Alaric's face twisted in horror as the truth hit him, a grim understanding dawning in his eyes. He clenched his fists, digging his fingers into the dirt, but no power surged through him, no energy answered his call. He was empty—stripped of the magic that had once been as natural to him as breathing.

"She... she left us like this," he said, bitterness lacing his words. "All that talk of being friends, and she just... took everything."

Mia shivered as Carol's parting words echoed faintly in her mind. *"It's because we're friends that you're allowed to live."* The memory of Carol's cold, triumphant gaze sent a chill down her spine, filling her with a mix of fear and anger. She pressed her hands to her temples, willing the memory away, but it clung to her like a shadow, refusing to let go.

"She's more dangerous now than... than Samantha ever was," Mia whispered, her voice trembling. "With our magic, she's stronger than any of them. We have to warn the others... before it's too late."

Alaric nodded, though he winced as he moved, the exhaustion and weakness pulling at his bones. "If she's willing to do this to us... there's no telling what she'll do to them. She's not... Carol anymore. Not the one we knew."

They struggled to their feet, leaning on each other for support, both of them feeling the terrible weight of what had been taken from them. They had lost not just their strength, but their very identities, the magic that had defined them stripped away, leaving them empty shells of who they had once been.

As they stumbled away from the clearing, the first light of dawn crept over the horizon, casting long shadows behind them. They knew they had to reach the others, to tell them what Carol had done. But with each step, Mia couldn't shake the feeling that they were too late—that something irreversible had already begun.

Chapter 22

Trixie was the first to spot them, two shadowed figures moving swiftly down the path toward the gate. Her eyes narrowed as she raised a hand, signalling the others. The faint morning light illuminated their faces as they drew closer, and Trixie recognized them as Mia and Alaric—members of the rogue coven. But something was wrong. Their steps were unsteady, their faces pale and drawn, and Carol was nowhere in sight.

"Stay back," Trixie murmured to the others, her gaze fixed on the approaching figures. She opened the gate just enough to allow them through, watching their every movement, ready for any sign of trouble. Mia and Alaric stumbled toward her, breathing heavily, their clothes dusted with dirt, and their eyes wide with fear.

"Where's Carol?" Trixie asked, her voice calm but laced with suspicion.

Mia shook her head, her face crumpling as she struggled to find her voice. "Carol... she—she betrayed us. She took everything." Her words were barely above a whisper, trembling as if saying them made the horror all too real.

Alaric stepped forward, his voice urgent. "We tried to stop her, but she—she's too powerful. She took all our magic." He looked down, his hands clenched into fists. "We're powerless."

Trixie's expression hardened as she took in their words. "She drained you both?" Her voice was low, a flash of anger in her eyes. "Where is she now?"

Mia and Alaric exchanged a look, fear etched deeply into their faces. "We don't know," Alaric said, his voice hoarse. "She left us there, unconscious. When we woke up... she was gone."

Trixie's gaze darted back down the path, half-expecting to see Carol materialize in the distance, her face twisted with newfound power. She looked back at Mia and Alaric, her expression grim. "You'd better come inside. Malory needs to hear this immediately."

The others gathered closer, their faces mirroring Trixie's alarm as she led the weakened pair through the gates and toward the coven's heart. As they walked, Mia and Alaric moved slowly, their steps faltering, as though the ground beneath them had become foreign and uncertain. The emptiness in their eyes unnerved Trixie; she could sense the absence of magic in them, a hollow where once there had been power and light.

Inside the coven hall, Malory and the Shadow Sisters awaited them, their expressions wary as Trixie escorted Mia and Alaric into the room. Malory's piercing gaze swept over them, her eyes narrowing as she sensed the unnatural void within them.

"What happened?" Malory demanded, her voice sharp, her gaze fixed on the two rogues. "Where is Carol?"

Mia swallowed, her voice barely above a whisper as she met Malory's intense stare. "She turned on us," she said, her voice breaking. "We thought she was going to help us—help us get revenge on the others. But instead... she used us. She took everything, drained all our magic... and left us like this." She looked down at her hands, her eyes empty. "She's more powerful than any of us now. More powerful than Samantha ever was."

The room fell silent, a heavy weight settling over them all. The Shadow Sisters exchanged uneasy glances, each of them sensing the magnitude of the threat that had been unleashed. Malory's expression remained cold, her mind working as she considered their options, but a flicker of something dangerous shone in her eyes.

"She's coming, isn't she?" Trixie murmured, her gaze fixed on Malory. "She'll come for us next."

Malory nodded slowly, her expression grave. "If Carol has taken the magic of two sorcerers, her power will be immense. She'll come for more—she won't stop until she has it all."

Mia shuddered, her voice trembling as she looked around at the assembled sisters. "You don't understand. She's... different now. Cold, ruthless. She looked at us like... like we were nothing."

Alaric nodded, his face pale. "It's going to take all of us—everyone we have—if we're going to have a chance at stopping her."

Malory's eyes glinted with steely resolve. "Then we'll be ready. Trixie, gather everyone. We don't have a moment to waste." She turned to Mia and Alaric, her gaze softening slightly as she looked at their weakened forms. "Rest, regain your strength. If Carol is as powerful as you say, we're going to need you both."

Trixie nodded, already moving to alert the others, her heart pounding with urgency. As she hurried from the room, a chilling certainty settled over her: Carol was coming, and they had only a narrow window to prepare for what would undoubtedly be the fiercest battle they had ever faced.

*

The coven members scrambled to prepare as Trixie relayed the grim news of Carol's betrayal. Malory's expression was grim as she issued orders, her voice sharp and commanding.

"Gather all available sorcerers and sorceresses. We need to fortify our defences immediately." She turned to Ember and Jade, the Shadow Sisters. "You two, work with Jade and Ember to set up layered shielding spells around the compound. We need to be ready for anything."

The sisters nodded, their faces etched with determination as they hurried to carry out Malory's instructions. Trixie moved to her side, her brow furrowed with worry.

"Do you truly think we can stop Carol, now that she's drained Mia and Alaric?" she murmured. "Her power must be immense."

Malory's jaw tightened. "We have no choice. If we don't stand against her now, she'll only grow stronger. Gather the most experienced sorcerers - we'll need to hit her with everything we have."

As the coven mobilized, a sense of grim determination settled over the group. They knew the stakes were higher than ever before. Carol's betrayal had revealed a ruthlessness they had never anticipated, and the thought of facing her with their full strength left them uneasy.

In the training grounds, the younger sorcerers worked quickly to erect layered barriers, weaving intricate patterns of light and energy that shimmered in the air. Ember and Jade coordinated their efforts, guiding them with calm, measured instructions.

"Remember, focus on stability and grounding," Jade called out. "The key is to create a solid foundation that can withstand even the most powerful assaults."

Jade and Ember oversaw the more experienced sorcerers as they prepared advanced defensive spells, their hands moving with practiced precision. Tendrils of energy coiled around the perimeter, creating a web of protection that pulsed with power.

Trixie and Malory observed the preparations, their expressions tense. They both knew that no matter how formidable their defences, Carol's newfound strength would put them to the test.

"I've gathered the most skilled sorcerers, as you requested," Trixie said, her voice low. "But I can't help but wonder if it will be enough."

Malory's gaze was fixed on the shimmering barriers, her brow furrowed in deep thought. "It has to be. We cannot afford to fail, not against an enemy as relentless and powerful as Carol."

A sudden, ominous rumble shook the ground, and the air crackled with an unseen energy. The sorcerers paused, their spells faltering as they looked around, fear etching their features.

Trixie's eyes widened. "She's here."

Malory's expression hardened, and she raised her staff, the gem at the tip flaring to life. "Positions, everyone! Prepare for battle!"

The coven members scrambled to their stations, their hands gripping their staves as they braced themselves for the onslaught. Ember and Jade reinforced the shielding spells, their voices rising in a chorus of incantations.

A deafening crack of energy rent the air, and a shimmering portal burst open at the far end of the training grounds. Through the swirling vortex, a figure emerged, her crimson gaze sweeping over the assembled sorcerers with a cold, calculating expression.

"Carol," Malory breathed, her voice tinged with a mixture of dread and determination.

Carol's lips curled into a cruel smile as she took in the sight of the coven's defences. "How... quaint," she purred, her voice dripping with disdain. With a casual flick of her wrist, she unleashed a torrent of dark energy, the power crackling through the air like lightning.

The sorcerers braced themselves, their staves raised as they channelled their magic into the shielding spells. But Carol's attack was relentless, battering against their defences with a force they had never encountered before.

Ember and Jade poured their energy into the barriers, their brows furrowed with concentration, but the strain was evident on their faces. The onslaught continued, each pulse of dark magic weakening the shields bit by bit.

Trixie and Malory joined the fray, their own spells interweaving with those of the other sorcerers, but even their combined power was no match for Carol's newfound strength.

"She's too powerful!" Jade cried, her voice strained. "I don't know how much longer we can hold her back!"

Malory's jaw tightened, her eyes narrowing as she focused her magic, pouring every ounce of her strength into reinforcing the shields. "We have to try! We cannot let her through!"

But Carol's relentless assault continued, the dark energy surging and swirling around the coven's defences. With a final, deafening crack, the barriers shattered, fragments of light and power scattering in all directions.

The sorcerers were flung backwards, their bodies slamming against the ground with bone-crushing force. Malory and Trixie fought to maintain their footing, their staves raised in a desperate attempt to counter Carol's attack.

"Impossible," Malory gasped, her eyes wide with disbelief. "How can she be this powerful?"

Carol's laughter, rich and chilling, echoed through the training grounds as she strode forward, her crimson gaze gleaming with triumph. "You fools," she sneered. "You thought you could stop me? I am unstoppable!"

With a casual flick of her wrist, she unleashed another devastating blast, sending the coven members hurtling through the air. Trixie ran, heading to the one person who might stand a chance against Carol's wrath, and Malory climbed to her feet, ready to withstand the onslaught and buy them more time.

She raised her hands, the air crackling with energy as she prepared to deliver the final, devastating blow. The sorceress braced herself, her faces etched with terror, knowing that she was powerless to stop her.

Chapter 23

The chaos in the training grounds was in full swing, with Carol's relentless assault overwhelming the coven's defences. Trixie, battered and weary from the earlier clash, broke away from the battle and hurried towards Samantha's cell, her expression etched with a mixture of panic and desperation.

Reaching the reinforced door, Trixie pressed her hand against the enchanted barrier, feeling the hum of ancient magic pulsing beneath her fingertips. "Samantha!" she cried, her voice laced with urgency. "Samantha, you have to help us!"

Inside the cell, Samantha looked up, her crimson gaze fixing on Trixie's anxious features. "Trixie? What's happening?"

"It's Carol," Trixie gasped, her words tumbling out in a rush. "She's turned on us, drained the power from Mia and Alaric, and now she's tearing us apart out there. We can't stop her, Samantha - we need your help!"

Samantha's brow furrowed, a flicker of unease crossing her features. "Carol has betrayed us?" She clenched her fists, the familiar rage beginning to stir within her. "Then let me out of here. I'll put an end to her madness."

Trixie's expression shifted to one of desperation. "I want to, Samantha, but I... I don't know how to take down the shields. This was powerful magic, ancient spell work - only the caster can undo it."

Samantha's gaze hardened as she pressed her hand against the glimmering barrier, feeling the weight of the enchantment pressing against her. "Then what do you suggest, Trixie? I can't just sit here while the Nepal crumbles around us."

Trixie's eyes widened, a sudden realization dawning on her. "Wait, Samantha - that's it! You have to absorb the magic from the shield, draw the power into yourself. If you can overload it, the barriers should collapse."

Samantha stared at her, a flicker of uncertainty crossing her features. "Absorb the magic? Can I even do that? It's very different than absorbing power from a crystal or a wand."

Trixie nodded, a note of conviction in her voice. "It is still a source of power, it just has different energy. You have to try. Your power has grown beyond anything we could have imagined. If anyone can do it, it's you."

Samantha's gaze hardened with determination, and she turned her attention back to the shimmering barrier. Closing her eyes, she focused her energy, feeling the hum of the enchantment pulsing against her skin. Slowly, she began to draw the power inward, channelling it through her core.

At first, the process was slow and arduous, the magic resisting her attempts. But as Samantha's concentration deepened, the resistance began to crumble, the energy flowing into her in a steady, pulsing stream.

Trixie watched in awe as Samantha's form began to glow, the crimson light building in intensity with each passing moment. The air crackled with the weight of the magic, and Trixie felt a shiver of unease run down her spine.

Suddenly, with a deafening crack, the barrier shattered, the shards of enchanted energy dissolving into the air. Samantha stood tall, her eyes burning with a fierce, unwavering determination.

"I'm ready, Trixie," she declared, her voice laced with a dangerous edge. "Let's go put an end to Carol's reign of terror."

Trixie hesitated for a moment, a flicker of guilt crossing her features. But then, with a resolute nod, she turned and led the way, Samantha striding behind her, the weight of her power palpable in the air.

The final confrontation was about to begin, and the fate of the Nepal hung in the balance.

As the coven members hastened to prepare their defences, a sudden, piercing wail shattered the tense silence. The air crackled with raw energy, and the very ground trembled beneath their feet.

Trixie spun around, her staff gripped tightly in her hand, her eyes widening in horror as a shimmering portal opened at the far end of the hall. Through the swirling vortex, a figure emerged, her crimson gaze sweeping over the assembled sorceresses with a terrifying calm.

"Carol," Malory breathed, her voice laced with dread, barely standing and blood spilled from every limb and wound.

But Carol's lips curved into a cruel smile, and with a casual flick of her wrist, she sent a torrent of dark energy surging toward them. The coven scrambled to erect their shields, but the power of Carol's attack was overwhelming, shattering their defences with ease.

As the sorceresses were flung backwards, Trixie watched in horror as Carol stepped through the portal, her laughter echoing through the chamber. The battle had only just begun, and the coven was hopelessly outmatched.

"If you won't stop her," Samantha murmured, her voice laced with a dangerous resolve, "then I will." She turned to Trixie, her face set with determination. "Give me a garnet. The bigger, the better."

Trixie frowned and dug deep into her pockets. "I... I have this. Is it big enough?"

It was the size of a kiwi fruit, which Samantha rolled it around in her hands. "It'll do." Then, raised it in front of her, ignoring the screams coming from outside. She muttered quietly, chanting a spell then shoved the orange garnet deep into her pocket for later.

Carol's cruel laughter echoed through the chamber as she stepped through the shimmering portal, her crimson gaze sweeping over the assembled sorceresses with a sense of unbridled power.

Samantha emerged from the crumbling remains of her cell, her body crackling with raw, untamed energy. Her eyes burned with a fierce determination as she faced down the woman who had betrayed them all.

"Carol," Samantha's voice was low and dangerous, "your reign of terror ends here."

Carol's lips curled into a mocking smile. "Oh, Samantha, how naive you are. My power is beyond anything you can comprehend." With a casual flick of her wrist, she unleashed a torrent of dark energy, the magic slamming into the coven's defences with devastating force.

The Sorceress' Claim

The sorceresses scrambled to erect their shields, but Carol's attacks were relentless, battering their spells with a power that left them reeling. Trixie and Malory fought to hold the line, but they could feel the strain of the onslaught weighing them down.

Amidst the chaos, Samantha surged forward, her crimson magic crackling to life as she met Carol's assault head-on. The two sorceresses clashed in a dazzling display of raw power, their spells colliding with earth-shaking force.

"You think you can stop me?" Carol hissed, her eyes narrowing as she poured more energy into her attacks. "The magic I've taken, it's mine now. All of it!"

Samantha gritted her teeth, her movements growing more frantic as she struggled to counter Carol's relentless barrage. "You're wrong, Carol. This power was never yours to take."

With a desperate surge of energy, Samantha unleashed a devastating blast, the crimson magic slamming into Carol and sending her hurtling backward. But the victory was short-lived, as Carol quickly regained her footing, her expression twisted with rage.

"Foolish girl," Carol spat, her hands glowing with a sickly, violet light. "You've only made me stronger."

She thrust her hands forward, and a swirling vortex of dark energy erupted from her palms, enveloping Samantha in a crushing embrace. Samantha cried out in pain as the magic sapped her strength, her body crumpling to the floor.

The coven members and Shadow Sisters watched in horror, their spells faltering as they witnessed Samantha's defeat. Malory's face was etched with a mixture of fear and determination.

"Samantha!" Maggie cried, her voice laced with anguish as she watched her friend fall.

But even as the darkness threatened to consume her, Samantha's lips curled into a faint, knowing smile. She clutched something tightly in her hand, her crimson gaze fixed on Carol.

"What's so amusing?" Carol demanded, her voice dripping with malice as she towered over Samantha's prone form. "Do you really think you can still win?"

Samantha's smile widened, and with a sudden, fluid motion, she raised her hand, revealing a large, gleaming garnet. "Because you've fallen right into my trap."

Before Carol could react, Samantha crushed the gem in her palm, and a blinding surge of energy erupted from the shattered crystal. The magic swirled and pulsed, gathering momentum as it hurtled back toward Carol.

The coven members and Shadow Sisters watched in stunned silence as the attack slammed into Carol, the dark sorceress crying out in anguish as the power of her own spell was turned against her. The violet energy that had once enveloped Samantha now engulfed Carol, draining her of her stolen strength.

Carol's eyes widened in horror as she felt the magic slipping away, her body growing weaker with each passing moment. "No, this can't be happening!" she screamed, her voice laced with a desperate panic.

Samantha struggled to her feet, her expression grim but resolute. "It's over, Carol. The power you stole is being returned to its rightful owner."

The Sorceress' Claim

As the last of Carol's stolen magic was pulled into the garnet, the dark sorceress collapsed to the ground, her body drained and lifeless. Samantha stood over her, the ancient gem pulsing with a crimson light in her hand.

The Shadow Sisters and coven members looked on in a mixture of awe and relief, their expressions shifting from despair to a cautious hope.

Malory stepped forward, her gaze fixed on the garnet in Samantha's hand. "What have you done, Samantha?"

Samantha's expression was solemn as she met Malory's gaze. "I've reclaimed what was mine, Malory. And now, the Nepal is safe from those who would seek to destroy it."

With a slow, deliberate motion, Samantha raised the garnet, the crimson light pulsing brighter with each passing moment. The others watched with bated breath, their hearts pounding as they realized the true nature of Samantha's plan.

As Samantha's fingers tightened around the gem, the Nepal seemed to hold its breath, the very air trembling with the weight of the magic that was about to be unleashed. And in that moment, they knew that the fate of their world hung in the balance, resting on the unwavering resolve of the sorceress who had once been their greatest threat.

Chapter 24

The training grounds fell silent, the air thick with tension as Samantha held the pulsing garnet in her hand. The assembled sorceresses and sorcerers held their breath, their gazes fixed on the powerful gem, waiting with bated breath to see what Samantha would do.

Samantha stared down at the crimson crystal, her expression unreadable as she weighed the power it contained. She could feel the energy thrumming within it, the promise of unimaginable strength whispering to her. It would be so easy to simply keep it, to wield the magic as her own.

Malory and the others watched Samantha with a mixture of trepidation and hope, their bodies tense and ready to react at the slightest movement. They had seen the destruction Samantha was capable of, the darkness that had nearly consumed her. And now, with the full might of the Raven Coven's stolen power within her grasp, they feared what she might do.

Slowly, Samantha lifted her gaze, her crimson eyes sweeping over the faces of the sorcerers and sorceresses. She could feel their eyes upon her, their fear and uncertainty palpable. For a moment, she wavered, the temptation to keep the power for herself almost overwhelming.

But then, her expression hardened with a newfound resolve. She turned to Ember, the leader of the Shadow Sisters, and held out the garnet, her hand unwavering.

"Take it," Samantha said, her voice calm and steady. "Keep it safe, and make sure it never falls into the wrong hands again."

Ember's eyes widened in surprise, her gaze flicking from the gem to Samantha's face. "Samantha, are you sure?" she asked, her voice barely above a whisper.

Samantha nodded, her lips curving into a faint, weary smile. "Yes. This power is too dangerous to be left in the hands of any one individual, even my own. It must be guarded, protected from those who would seek to abuse it."

Ember hesitated for a moment, then reached out and gently took the garnet from Samantha's outstretched hand. The moment her fingers closed around the gem, a ripple of energy pulsed through the air, and the sorcerers and sorceresses exhaled a collective sigh of relief.

Malory stepped forward, her expression a mixture of respect and admiration. "Samantha, you have shown remarkable wisdom and restraint. The Nepal owes you a debt of gratitude."

Samantha inclined her head, her gaze meeting Malory's. "The Nepal has suffered enough on my account. This is the least I can do to make amends."

The Shadow Sisters and coven members exchanged grateful looks, their once-tense postures relaxing as the immediate threat of Samantha's power being misused faded. Maggie and Ethan moved to Samantha's side, their faces etched with a mixture of pride and relief.

"Samantha, we..." Maggie began, her voice trembling with emotion. "We're so proud of you."

Ethan nodded, a genuine smile tugging at the corners of his lips. "You've come so far. We knew you could do it."

Samantha's expression softened, and she reached out to squeeze Maggie's hand, a gesture that spoke volumes more than any words could. In that moment, the weight of her past transgressions seemed to lift, and she felt a sense of peace settle over her.

The Nepal had been spared, and Samantha knew that her journey, though fraught with darkness and betrayal, had led her to this point – a place where she could finally begin to heal, and to forge a new path forward, one where she would use her power to protect, rather than destroy.

As Ember and the Shadow Sisters secured the garnet, the coven members and sorceresses began to regroup, their expressions filled with a renewed sense of hope and determination. The battle may have been won, but they knew that the work of rebuilding and healing was only just beginning.

As the coven members and Shadow Sisters began to regroup, organizing their efforts to rebuild and secure the Nepal, Malory and Trixie exchanged a troubled glance. They turned to Samantha, their expressions cautious and uncertain.

"Samantha," Malory began, her voice measured, "we couldn't help but notice that you were able to escape your cell. And if I'm not mistaken, that was a powerful enchantment, one that only the caster could have broken."

Samantha nodded, a faint smile tugging at the corners of her lips. "Yes, that's correct. I absorbed the magic from the shield, drawing it into myself until the barriers fell."

The leaders shared a worried look, the implication of Samantha's actions weighing heavily upon them. Trixie cleared her throat, her gaze flicking nervously to the garnet that Ember still clutched in her hand.

"Then, if you were able to overcome such a potent spell so easily..." Trixie's voice trailed off, the unspoken concern hanging in the air.

Samantha's expression darkened as she recognized the direction of their thoughts. "I know what you're thinking," she said, her voice laced with a warning. "And it's a bad idea."

Malory's brow furrowed, her eyes narrowing as she studied the powerful sorceress. "Samantha, if there is a way to... contain your power, to ensure the safety of the Nepal—"

"No," Samantha cut her off, her tone firm and unyielding. "You cannot use that crystal against me. It was my magic that was bound to it, and only I can control its power. Trying to use it to subdue me would only result in you losing your own abilities."

The leaders fell silent, their faces etched with a mixture of fear and resignation. They knew that Samantha was right - the garnet, once a weapon against her, was now a double-edged sword that they dared not wield.

Ember stepped forward, her expression grave. "Samantha, we understand your concern. But you must see our perspective. Your power is... unprecedented. If it were to ever slip from your control again, the consequences could be catastrophic."

Samantha's gaze hardened, and she straightened her posture, her crimson eyes burning with a fierce determination. "I've already made my choice," she declared, her voice ringing with a sense of finality. "I will use my power to protect the Nepal, not to destroy it. You'll have to trust that I've learned from my mistakes."

The thought of entrusting such immense abilities to a single individual, even one who had proven their loyalty, filled them with a deep-seated apprehension.

Maggie and Ethan moved to Samantha's side, their expressions resolute. "We believe in her," Maggie said, her voice unwavering. "Samantha has proven that she's in control, that she's on our side. Trying to contain her power, to treat her like a threat, will only push her away."

"Look," Samantha sighed, the heavy reluctance hung on her shoulders. "I can see that none of you are going to trust me, so maybe it's best if I just leave. I'll go to the mountains or something. Away from people."

"But we do trust you!" Maggie piped up, smiling, though it didn't reach her eyes.

"Yeah well," Samantha said, shrugging. "The problem is, I don't trust you. You betrayed me already. You were my best friend. I can't forgive you. And I can't forgive Ethan."

"Please," Trixie pleaded. "Stay?"

Samantha shook her head. "I'm sorry. I can't. Besides, I think Nepal has been put through enough." She grabbed a bag and hauled it on her shoulders. She was going to need to pack a few things before leaving. "It's for the best."

Chapter 25

Samantha could sense the lingering unease in the eyes of the coven leaders and Shadow Sisters as they regarded her.

"Samantha, you can't be serious," Maggie breathed, her voice laced with anguish. "After everything we've been through, you can't just leave us now."

Ethan nodded, his brow furrowed with a mixture of worry and confusion. "Where will you go? What will you do?"

Samantha turned to them, her expression softening as she reached out to squeeze their hands. "I'm going to a remote area, far from the prying eyes of the coven and the Nepal. There, I can focus on honing my abilities, on learning to control this power that has brought so much chaos." She offered them a faint, reassuring smile. "And I'll be there, if you ever need me. But for now, I need you to trust that this is the right decision."

Malory stepped forward, her gaze searching Samantha's face. "And you truly believe this is the best course of action?" Her voice was laced with a hint of scepticism, but also a grudging respect.

Samantha met her gaze steadily. "I do. This way, you won't have to worry about my power slipping from my control. I can focus on my own growth, and you can focus on rebuilding the Nepal without the constant shadow of my past looming over you."

The coven leaders exchanged a weighted look, their expressions troubled. But after a moment, Malory inclined her head in a gesture of reluctant acceptance.

"Very well, Samantha. If this is your decision, then we will respect it." She paused, a flicker of something akin to gratitude crossing her features. "And we thank you, for your honesty, and for your willingness to put the needs of the Nepal above your own."

Samantha nodded, a faint smile tugging at the corners of her lips. "Thank you, Malory. I know it's not an easy decision, but it's the right one - for all of us."

As Samantha turned to depart, Maggie and Ethan moved to her side, their faces etched with a mixture of sadness and understanding.

"We'll miss you, Samantha," Maggie murmured, her voice trembling slightly.

With that, Samantha turned and strode away, her crimson gaze fixed on the horizon. The coven members and Shadow Sisters watched her go, a sense of bittersweet resignation settling over them. They knew that Samantha's departure was a necessary step, a sacrifice that would ensure the safety of their world.

*

Samantha moved through her small living quarters, packing the few belongings she had accumulated during her time in the coven. She gathered some provisions for the journey ahead, her mind already focused on the remote, secluded location she had chosen to make her new home.

As she slung the pack over her shoulder, Samantha paused, her gaze settling on the framed photograph by her bedside. It was an image of her and her mother, taken before the darkness had consumed her life. With a wistful sigh, she tucked the frame carefully into her bag, determined to hold onto that precious reminder of her past.

Stepping out into the dimly lit corridor, Samantha made her way to the main entrance, where she knew her mother would be waiting to say her goodbyes. The older woman stood there, her eyes glistening with unshed tears, as she pulled Samantha into a tight embrace.

"My dear, I'm going to miss you so," her mother murmured, her voice thick with emotion. "But I understand why you must do this. Just promise me you'll be safe, and that you'll come back to me, someday."

Samantha returned the embrace, her own eyes softening with a touch of regret. "I promise, Mother. This isn't goodbye forever - just a necessary step on my journey."

As they parted, Samantha offered her mother a reassuring smile, squeezing her hand gently before turning to make her way out of the coven's compound. But as she reached the gates, a familiar sight caught her eye, and she felt her steps falter.

Maggie and Ethan were approaching, their hands clasped together, their expressions a mixture of sadness and uncertainty. Samantha's gaze flickered down to their entwined fingers, and she couldn't help but feel a pang of bitterness at the sight.

Sensing her scrutiny, Maggie and Ethan quickly let go of each other's hands, their faces flushing with embarrassment. Samantha let out a weary sigh, meeting their gazes with a measure of resignation.

"Samantha, we..." Maggie began, her voice trembling, "we just wanted to say goodbye. And... and we're so sorry, for everything."

Ethan nodded, his own expression etched with remorse. "We know we can never make up for what we did to you, but we want you to know that we care about you, Samantha."

Samantha studied them, her features softening slightly. "I appreciate the sentiment, I truly do. But I can't forgive you, but I - I don't hate you either. Truly, I'm no longer consumed by the pain of your betrayal."

She paused, her gaze hardening ever so slightly. "However, that doesn't mean I've forgotten what you did. If you had come to me, told me the truth, it would have been painful, yes. But nothing compared to the anguish you put me through by choosing to betray me instead."

Maggie and Ethan exchanged a guilty look, their shoulders slumping with the weight of Samantha's words.

"You should have left me, Ethan," Samantha continued, her voice tinged with a hint of regret. "You should have told me that your heart belonged to Maggie. It would have hurt, but at least I would have known the truth."

Without waiting for their response, Samantha adjusted the strap of her pack and turned to continue on her way.

Samantha strode through the gates, disappearing into the shadowy landscape beyond, leaving Maggie and Ethan to watch her go, their expressions etched with a mixture of sorrow and resignation.

*

Samantha moved silently through the dense forest, her steps light and her senses alert. Gone were the confines of the coven's compound, replaced by the vast, untamed wilderness that stretched out before her. The air was crisp and cool, the gentle breeze carrying the earthy scent of moss and damp soil.

As she walked, Samantha occasionally paused to pluck a ripe berry or fruit from the surrounding bushes and trees, her fingers nimble and her gaze discerning. With a thought, she conjured a small flame to boil water from a nearby stream, using the roots of various weeds to create a simple but nourishing tea.

Throughout her journey, Samantha took great care to hide her tracks, her magic swirling around her like an invisible cloak. She had no intention of being followed or ambushed, not when she had finally found the solace she so desperately needed.

As the sun began to dip below the horizon, Samantha found herself standing at the base of the rugged mountain range, the peaks rising before her like ancient sentinels. A faint smile tugged at the corners of her lips as she felt the brisk, cold air caress her face, a welcome change from the stifling confines of the Nepal she had left behind.

Raising her hands, Samantha summoned her magic, the crimson energy pulsing and swirling around her. With a fluid motion, she directed the power into the mountainside, shaping and moulding the rock and earth to her will. Slowly, a large, cavernous opening began to emerge, the rough walls smoothing and hardening into a solid, protective shelter.

Samantha stepped inside, her gaze sweeping over the spacious, dimly lit expanse. With a flick of her wrist, she summoned a barrier of ice, sealing the entrance and locking out the outside world. The cave was now her domain, a place where she could focus on honing her abilities without the constant weight of the coven's scrutiny and the Nepal's troubles.

As she settled down on the cool, smooth surface, Samantha felt a sense of peace wash over her. The journey had been long, the challenges daunting, but she had emerged from the darkness, her power tempered, and her resolve strengthened. No longer would she be a pawn in others' games, a weapon to be wielded and controlled.

Here, in this remote, secluded sanctuary, Samantha would forge her own path, her own destiny.

The flickering light of the fire cast dancing shadows across the walls, and Samantha allowed herself a moment of quiet reflection.

With a deep breath, she settled deeper into her makeshift bed, her crimson gaze fixed on the icy barrier that shielded her from the outside world. Tomorrow would bring new trials, new lessons to be learned, but for now, Samantha was content to simply exist in the tranquillity of her own solitude, her power humming with a newfound sense of purpose.

Epilogue

Six months had passed since Samantha's departure, and the Nepal had slowly begun to heal and rebuild in her absence. The coven and Shadow Sisters had worked tirelessly to mend the damage wrought by the devastating battle, their combined efforts restoring hope and stability to the once-shattered realm.

One day, as Malory and Trixie were engaged in a quiet discussion over a cup of tea, a small group of young witches approached them, their expressions cautious but determined.

"Forgive the intrusion," the leader of the group, a petite woman with vibrant green eyes, began. "But we've come to offer our assistance in the ongoing recovery efforts."

Malory regarded them with a curious gaze, setting down her teacup. "Your help is most welcome. We've been grateful for the work you've done in caring for those wounded in the attack."

The young witch nodded, a faint smile tugging at her lips. "It's the least we could do, after all that happened. We owe Samantha a debt of gratitude, even if the cost was high."

Trixie's brow furrowed slightly at the mention of Samantha's name, but she remained silent, allowing the young woman to continue.

"However, there is something else we've come to discuss," the witch said, her expression growing more serious. "While tending to the injured, we came across a prophet - a witch with a gift for divination. She... she has foreseen trouble on the horizon."

Malory and Trixie exchanged a weighted look, the gravity of the situation settling over them.

"Trouble?" Malory prompted, her voice even. "What kind of trouble?"

The young witch hesitated, her gaze flickering between the two coven leaders. "She said... she said the trouble would come with the first sign of spring."

The room fell silent, the weight of the witch's words hanging in the air. Malory's expression hardened, her fingers tightening around her teacup.

"Then we must be vigilant," she declared, her voice laced with a newfound urgency. "Inform the others and have them ready to respond at a moment's notice. We cannot afford to be caught unawares again."

Trixie nodded in agreement, her own features etched with a mixture of concern and determination. "And perhaps... it may be time to send word to Samantha, to bring her back into the fold. Her power could be the key to our survival, should this prophecy prove true."

The young witch's eyes widened slightly, a hint of apprehension crossing her features. "Samantha? But after all that's happened, do you think she would return?"

Malory's gaze was unwavering as she considered the question. "If the Nepal is truly in peril, then we must do whatever it takes to ensure its safety. And Samantha has proven herself a fierce protector, when the need arises."

With a solemn nod, the young witch turned to leave, her companions trailing behind her. As they disappeared into the shadows, Malory and Trixie exchanged a weighted look, the unspoken worry etched into their features.

The first signs of spring were on the horizon, and with them, the promise of a new challenge that would test the very limits of the Nepal's resilience. And this time, they knew that they might need Samantha's power, her unwavering determination, to see them through the trials that lay ahead.

About the Author

My name is Michelle, and I am from England UK. I have been writing since high school, but didn't start taking it more seriously as an author until my eldest daughter was born. I have enjoyed every minute, and I have no plans to stop.

I wrote my first book in 2009, and this is my 30th book.

I am looking forward to exploring more genres and write more stories for you all to enjoy!

If you want to join my newsletter, you can find me on https://crazyassedwriter.substack.com.

Happy Reading!

Milton Keynes UK
Ingram Content Group UK Ltd.
UKHW030848151124
451262UK00001B/346